CW01494971

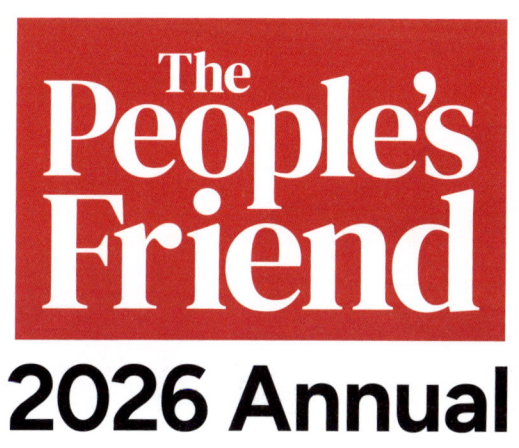

2026 Annual

COOLEY PENINSULA, IRELAND

THE Cooley Peninsula, often overlooked by travellers, offers everything from natural beauty to national historic significance. With winding roads, stunning coastal views and rich cultural heritage, this region is a top spot for visitors interested in Ireland's past.

A scenic drive along the coast allows visitors to explore towns like Carlingford, with its castles and bustling harbour.

The area is also known for its delicious seafood, particularly oysters and mussels, which are farmed in the pristine waters of Carlingford Lough.

As you head deeper into the peninsula, there are fascinating historical sites, such as the Long Woman's Grave. This ancient monument is said to be the grave of a seven-foot Spanish woman who married a local chieftain's son.

He showed her the land that she had married into and she was so disappointed that she died on the spot.

Contents

Complete Stories

Dear Readers

Hello and welcome to "The People's Friend Annual". We're delighted to present a selection of heartwarming stories, which have been carefully selected just for you. There's 25 brand-new tales, written by many of your "Friend" favourites. These stories of joy and romance, and just a little bit of drama, are sure to entertain you. Throughout your annual, you will also find some truly wonderful poetry and interesting trivia. There's even fascinating facts about animals! I do hope you find time to sit back and relax with this lovely collection of words and artwork.

Stuart Johnstone, Editor.

Set in **1955**

109

121

127

Pages Of Joy

BY ALISON WASSELL

EVERYTHING looks so drab now we've taken the decorations down."

I seal the box of baubles with packing tape, feeling as bleak as the weather.

I know some people see January as the chance for a fresh start, but it's my least favourite time of year.

There are weeks of dark mornings and evenings stretching ahead and no family birthdays to look forward to until the spring.

"It might be easier if there was something to celebrate," I say.

My husband, Jamie, looks up from the bumper puzzle book he received for Christmas.

"Have a look on the internet," he says. "Practically every day seems to be national something or other day. You could choose one of them to celebrate."

He's half-joking, but the torrential rain has scuppered my plans for a walk, so I get my laptop out.

I've already missed National Science-fiction Day and World Braille Day.

"Here's one you might enjoy," I say when I discover that Global Wordsearch Day is on the 16th of this month.

"Every day is wordsearch day, as far as I'm concerned," he replies with a chuckle.

I carry on scrolling – and then, I find it.

January 18 is Winnie-The-Pooh Day.

Jamie, who even as a boy never read anything but non-fiction, looks unimpressed.

But "Winnie-The-Pooh" was my favourite book when I was a little girl, and I can still quote chunks of it verbatim.

Further research reveals that this year it will be exactly 100 years since it was published.

"I'm just looking for something," I shout when John asks, an hour later, why it's taking so long to put the decorations away.

He's not good on ladders, so he always stands at the bottom holding ours steady while I go into the loft.

Any minute now I know he'll start fretting about missing the start of one of his TV quiz shows.

I'm about to give up my search and come down when my eyes rest on a battered cardboard box with *Books To Keep* scrawled in black marker pen on the side.

"Eureka!" I cry.

"Well, at least you've cheered up," Jamie says as I carefully pass it through the loft hatch.

The contents of the box keep me happily occupied for the rest of the afternoon.

"Winnie-The-Pooh" is not the only treasure I rediscover.

There is the hardback copy of

Illustration: Pat Gregory.

Noel Streatfeild's "Ballet Shoes" that my parents gave me for my ninth birthday, a pile of tatty Enid Blyton paperbacks and several "Jackie" annuals.

But it's Pooh I'm really interested in.

In my mind I travel back in time to when Mum and Dad read the book to me at bedtime, often arguing over whose turn it was, and then my excitement, a year or so later, when I realised I could read it for myself.

It was probably the very first chapter book I ever tackled.

Now, as I turn the pages, I think how much nicer the original E.H. Shepard illustrations are than the Disney version.

I recall how I longed to explore the Hundred Acre Wood with Pooh and his friends.

I'm still lost in thought when my phone rings.

"Of course we'd love to have Myla to stay," I say after chatting for a bit. "We don't get to see nearly enough of her."

Listening to my half of the conversation, Jamie grins.

He loves spending time with our granddaughter as much as I do and hates the fact that she and her parents live so far away.

Having her to ourselves for a whole weekend while our daughter and son-in-law go to see a West End show will be a treat for both of us.

January has definitely taken a turn for the better.

I hand the phone to Jamie so that he can chat to Lorna.

"Your mother's had her nose stuck in a dusty old book all afternoon," I hear him grumble.

"It's perfect timing!" I say afterwards. "Winnie-The-Pooh day falls on the Sunday. We'll be able to celebrate it with Myla."

Jamie pulls one of his faces.

"I hope you're not planning to spend the entire time reading," he says. "I'm sure she'd have more fun at the science museum."

Of course, what he really means is that he'd love to go to the science museum.

"If you're good, we can go there on the Saturday," I promise.

The following week I go into town and buy copies of "Winnie-The-Pooh" and "The House At Pooh Corner" for Myla.

When I get home, I wrap them in teddy-bear-covered paper and add a gift tag.

I hope you enjoy these as much as I did. Love from Granny, it says.

I feel bad about not adding Jamie's name, but this is a special gift just from me.

"You should give her something, too," I tell him.

He spends ages on his computer, and the next day a package arrives.

It's a Pooh-themed LEGO set.

"Myla and I can assemble it together when she gets bored with her book," he explains with a twinkle in his eye.

I'm not expecting there to be much time for LEGO, not with all the activities I have planned.

"I've found a Pooh-shaped biscuit cutter online," I tell him. "I

thought we could do some baking in the morning, then if the weather's fine we could take a picnic to the park and pretend it's the wood.

"Or we might even be able to find a bridge over a stream where we can play Poohsticks."

I have to explain to Jamie what Poohsticks is.

"So you throw a stick over a bridge, and wait for it to come out on the other side?" he says. "Do you think she'll be interested in that?

"Childhood's a lot different now from how it was in our day, Marian," he adds.

"She'll love it," I assure him, although he's managed to sow a seed of doubt in my mind.

We Facetime our granddaughter every week and see her every few months, but we don't know her nearly as well as we'd like to.

This will be the longest time she's ever spent with us, and the first time she's stayed over without her parents.

I want it to be perfect.

When she arrives on the Friday evening, she has already changed into her pyjamas in the car and is fast asleep.

Her dad carries her upstairs and she doesn't stir as we tuck her into bed.

At seven o'clock the next morning she is full of energy and raring to go, bouncing on our bed like Tigger.

"Grandad's been on his best behaviour these last few weeks, so I think we should take him to the museum as a reward," I tell her.

She looks unsure, until Jamie

mentions that there are dinosaurs.

She says she's done dinosaurs at school.

"What's your favourite, Grandad? Mine's the brachiosaurus, because it has a long neck like a giraffe," she says, and from then on there's no stopping them.

They chat away all through breakfast and the car journey, exchanging dinosaur facts.

I feel a bit left out, because the only dinosaur I can identify with any confidence is the T-rex.

But it's lovely seeing the two of them enjoying each other's company.

The day is a great success.

After the dinosaurs we go to the planetarium, where there is a special live show for children, although Jamie and I enjoy it as much as Myla does.

Then, of course, there is the obligatory visit to the café for something to eat, and to the gift shop, where we treat her to a

WHEN BILLY WAS A KID

Back before the Beatles,
When Billy was a kid,
Do you remember all the fun we had
And all the things we did?
Ringing neighbours' doorbells
And running down the street
Until our mothers called us in
When it was time to eat.
We thought we'd never grow up,
But all too soon we did.
I bet you'd like to go back to
When Billy was a kid

Julia Douglas

Illustration: Shutterstock.

➤ cuddly brachiosaurus, because it's not often that we get to spoil her.

"That was the best day ever," Myla says as she snuggles up in bed with her dinosaur, who she has named Brian.

"Tomorrow will be even better," I promise as I kiss her goodnight.

We wake in the morning to gale-force winds and rain battering the windows.

There will be no picnic in the park or Poohsticks.

"This storm wasn't meant to arrive until this evening," I say indignantly.

I could kick myself for not having devised a back-up plan.

"Well, you can still make the biscuits. And indoor picnics can be fun, too," Jamie points out.

He's right, but Myla has baked with me before, and there's nothing particularly magical about sitting on our living-room floor.

Still, perhaps her presents will keep her entertained.

"Happy Winnie-The-Pooh Day," I say when I go to wake her.

The day at the museum must have tired her out.

Sleepily, she rubs her eyes and, for a moment, she doesn't seem to know where she is or what on earth I'm talking about.

"Are we going on an adventure?" she asks.

"Well, sort of," I reply, reasoning to myself that reading a good book is a kind of adventure.

I offer honey on toast for breakfast because I'm sure that's what Pooh would have had.

Myla asks if we have any chocolate spread.

We don't and she has to settle for a poached egg.

"I'll get some in for next time you come," I say, wondering when that will be.

When breakfast is over, I tell Myla we have some presents for her.

Immediately, she brightens up.

"It's like having an extra birthday," she says, excitedly ripping the paper off the LEGO set.

She's delighted and wants to make a start on it right away.

Jamie is equally keen.

"What about this one?" I ask, handing her my gift.

Her face falls.

"Books," she says, failing to hide her disappointment.

"Not just any old books. These are stories I loved when I was your age. I thought we could read them together."

"Thanks, Granny. I'll look at them later. I don't really like reading much."

After a cursory glance she puts them aside and turns back to the LEGO, which Jamie has already made a start on.

Two hours later they're still at it.

I ask Myla if she'd like to make biscuits with me.

"I'd rather finish this," she says, so I wander off to the kitchen to prepare the picnic.

I produce cheese sandwiches shaped like bees, cheese straws that are meant to represent Poohsticks, a tray of salad vegetables arranged to look like Rabbit's garden and, of course, the Pooh-shaped biscuits.

Myla loves it, even though she has no idea what any of it is meant to be.

"Mum and Dad will be here to collect you soon," Jamie says afterwards. "I think it would be nice if you looked at those books with Granny before you go home."

Reluctantly she agrees, so we curl up together on the sofa.

"How about we take it in turns to read a page?" I suggest, but Myla isn't keen.

"You read and I'll just listen," she tells me.

So that's what we do.

I read and read, and I am carried back to that lovely, innocent world inhabited by Pooh, Piglet, Eeyore, Rabbit, Owl and Christopher Robin.

It takes me some time to realise that Myla isn't really listening.

Her thumb is in her mouth and, clutching Brian the dinosaur, she looks much younger than her six years.

"Aren't you enjoying it, darling?" I ask gently.

She looks up at me, her eyes full of tears.

"I'm not good at reading, Granny. That's why I didn't want to do it."

She buries her face in my cardigan and I stroke her hair.

"I'll let you into a little secret," I say. "When your mummy was your age, I remember her saying the same thing. Then she found a book about penguins in the library and there was no stopping her."

Of course, it wasn't as simple as that.

Memories of how Jamie and I worried about how Lorna seemed to be falling behind her classmates come flooding back.

But in the end it turned out that all she needed was something that really interested her to make everything click into place.

"Maybe this isn't the book for you," I say. "You'll find something you want to read about soon enough."

Myla holds up Brachiosaurus Brian.

"I'd like to read a story about him," she says.

That's when I get one of my brilliant ideas.

I tell her all about how A.A. Milne wrote the Pooh stories for his little boy.

"Maybe I could write some Brian-The-Brachiosaurus books for you," I suggest.

Myla's eyes light up.

"Really, Granny? I'd love to read those," she says, giving me a hug.

It takes me a lot of research and another visit to the museum for inspiration, much to Jamie's delight.

But two months later I have typed up my first story and printed it out.

Jamie, revealing an artistic talent he has kept secret all these years, adds some illustrations.

"Is it ready?" Myla asks the minute she bursts through the door, here for another weekend visit.

At bedtime, she follows the words with her finger as I read them.

Halfway through, she squeezes my hand.

"Can I have a turn at reading now, Granny?" she asks.

I hand the book over to her and, with very little help from me, that's exactly what she does. ∎

A Touch Of Silver

The cornflower skies of morning
Are giving way to grey,
But one small patch of brightness
Brings promise to the day.

For clouds are touched with silver
Despite the threat of rain –
A heavenly reminder
That hope is not in vain.

Storms are only fleeting,
And dark as they may seem,
There'll be a touch of silver,
So hold fast to your dream!

It may not lie within your grasp,
It may still take some time –
The view from every mountain top
Is surely worth the climb.

Look for the touch of silver
When faith is burning low.
Tomorrow may hold brighter skies
Than you could ever know!

Marian Cleworth

Illustration: Shutterstock.

MACROSTY PARK BANDSTAND, CRIEFF.

THE charming town of Crieff, hometown of Scottish actor Ewan McGregor, is nestled in the foothills of the Highlands.

A visit to the historic Glenturret Distillery, Scotland's oldest working distillery, is a must. You can join one of the daily tours and learn about the whisky-making process and even sample the local spirit.

Crieff's rich history is intertwined with local legends and folklore. The town is associated with the infamous Kate McNiven, a figure from Scottish folklore who was accused of witchcraft.

The MacRosty Bandstand was built by a Glaswegian foundry and installed in 1906 to provide the locals with entertainment.

The Right Type

BY JACKIE MORRISON

THE student party was all set up.

There was no alcohol, just an urn bought for the occasion together with a bowl of tea bags and a jar of instant coffee.

A coffee machine would have been too much hissing noise for the evening ahead, although nothing could be louder than the manual typewriter keys hitting the roller.

For the most part, Colin, the shop owner of The Right Type, discouraged people from touching the typewriters at all.

The vintage machines deserved respect, especially after the painstaking hours of work to restore them to their original working order.

It only took one over-enthusiastic visitor to mash the keys or ruin a ribbon.

Colin could usually identify the genuine customers; the people who were interested in particular models.

Others treated the shop like a curiosity, a museum.

Tonight, it was anything but a museum, although the nostalgic smell of metal and ink held everything together.

Colin felt discombobulated at the chatter that was rising and falling like a dance to accompany the beat of typewriter keys.

The door of The Right Type was open to appear welcoming and to prevent those inside the crowded basement shop from feeling claustrophobic.

Stone steps rose to the Edinburgh street above them, and through the black iron railings, they could see the feet and legs of commuters strutting towards the bus and tram stops just up the road.

It had been an ideal location for his grandparents' deli shop, but they had retired years ago, leaving Colin to inherit the property.

He'd taken his time to clear it out and restructure the layout, creating a workshop at the rear and space in the main shop to display rows of typewriters visible from the double bay windows.

To make the grade here, they had to be in immaculate working

Illustration: David Young.

order with no sticky keys, and Colin was a dab hand at bringing them back to life.

These days, Colin conducted a lot of his business over the internet, but he used the shop as his showcase.

Amy, who was completing a creative writing MA at Edinburgh University, had turned her hand to decorating an A-frame blackboard in multi-pastel shades of chalk, inviting people down to the Poets Night/Poets Type.

Going by the numbers, her efforts had worked.

The little shop overflowed with people, like a burst cushion.

It put Colin on edge a little, but Amy had been reassuring.

"Colin, relax! The typewriters weigh a ton. Nobody's going to steal one and run down Princes Street with it!"

It made him chuckle to visualise Spud and Renton, from the Irvine Welsh movie "Trainspotting", running along the famous Edinburgh main street with a typewriter under each of their arms.

How did she always know what he was thinking?

Amy had been a godsend.

A local student and poet, she had been a regular volunteer, typing in the window every Wednesday, and had encouraged Colin to set up his social media pages.

This evening had been her idea.

Creative-writing students mingled with other customers and newbies, approaching the table where Amy had settled her grandmother Eliza, who had agreed to help by typing mini-poems or love letters tonight.

They offered every visitor a "free" poem with a donation to the fund-raising bucket, which would buy books to donate to a children's charity.

Colin found it amusing to see that Eliza had brought her own portable typewriter.

He looked around the shop.

Were there not enough typewriters here for her to choose from?

But he understood. Familiarity with the strike of the keys, the exact pressure and touch required, the muscle memory of finding the return lever . . .

She knew what she was doing.

Had Amy suggested her grandma come dressed as a 1950s-type secretary?

If so, she was the most glamorous secretary Colin had ever seen.

She was wearing a cotton dress with a defined waist and short sleeves. It was mid-calf length, showing off her slim legs and blue leather pumps that matched the little red flower pattern of her blue dress.

Eliza's skin was impossibly peachy with freckles. Either she gardened or had been in sunnier climes.

Colin felt like porridge next to her. He barely saw the sun.

He walked quickly from his third-floor flat on Frederick Street down to the shop each day, his head down, hat on, every inch of skin covered, even in summer.

Summer was what she smelled like – like flowers of some sort.

He didn't know flowers at all.

Eliza was like a tall vase filled with opulent, flouncy petals – the sort people stare at and florists charge a fortune for.

Her smile wasn't wrinkles, crinkles, teeth and round cheeks; her smile was connection and curiosity.

He longed for her to see him, to look at him the way she looked at others.

These students were enthralled by her.

"Tell me about your dog," Eliza said to a young man.

Her head tilted as she listened, and the shy young guy broke into a smile as she offered some words, her eyebrows question marks, confirming what she was to write or rather type.

This woman belonged here tonight. And every other night, he wished.

Summer was what she smelled like – like flowers of some sort

"Colin, come meet my gran!" Amy grabbed Colin's arm.

He wasn't ready. He wanted to keep watching her, to indulge in being an observer, but Amy led him forward.

Feeling every bit like the shy young student he once was, he stopped Amy by pulling back on her arm to save them interrupting Eliza.

Hands held like a pianist, her wrists suspended as her fingers were doing the work, she looked like she was watching a movie in her head.

Her eyes were looking towards the shelves in the back of the shop, lined with typewriters in blue, green, red, maroon and cream, their carriages smiling.

With a flourish, she pulled the piece out.

The blue ribbon was almost violet in the light. A cursive script font.

To Colin, the lines on the paper resembled art.

He had supplied a quality conqueror paper with a watermark.

Eliza held the next piece of paper up to the light to ensure she'd insert it the right way up.

Colin sighed with delight.

"Gran, this is the shop owner, Colin.," Amy introduced. "Colin, this is my grandma, Eliza."

Colin felt shaken out of his revere.

"Eliza," he repeated and held Eliza's hand.

She had neatly manicured fingers with natural nails, and her hand had been warmed by the manual typing.

He placed his other hand on top and it felt as if he were creating a large ball of white light between their hands.

"Eliza. You type beautifully," he told her. "You're welcome to try any of my typewriters – all of them, in fact.

"I love yours, too" he went on. "It's a great specimen. I'd love you to come every day."

Amy laughed and pulled on Colin's arm.

"Colin, Gran has a queue."

Eliza smiled and bent her head towards Colin.

"It seems I have some typing to do. Amy is making up the poems and I'm helping."

"Yes," Colin replied and moved backwards, calling to Eliza's back as he did so.

"That's a beautiful model. The Olivetti Valentine is much sought after. It's a design icon and in stunning condition!"

He screwed up his eyes.

If only he didn't sound so awkward all the time, especially right now . . .

Eliza smiled and stroked the red case.

"It's been with me every place I've ever lived," he told him.

"I'd love to hear all about that," Colin spluttered. "Where the typewriter has been, where you have been . . .

"Perhaps you can visit the shop again tomorrow."

Eliza looked into his eyes and the rest of the busy shop receded as she spoke.

"I'm thinking about coming in every Wednesday with Amy." She smiled. "I have a coffee pot and teapot in need of a new home, along with some porcelain cups and saucers. I think they'd suit your events."

"That is very kind of you," Colin returned. "And, um, maybe I could make you a cup of tea or coffee?"

He floundered and Amy nudged his elbow.

"Maybe a pot of tea at the Balmoral Hotel would be a nice place for a chat?" she suggested. "Or an afternoon tea? I can mind the shop for a few hours. Maybe Friday?"

Colin felt sweat on his brow.

"You would mind the shop?" he whispered.

"I would." Amy nodded conspiratorially. "I think you'll have a lot to share.

"Gran has lots of stories about her travels and her books. And you know all about her typewriter."

Then Amy's voice dropped to a whisper.

"Gran was a secretary in the Foreign Office and worked in lots of different posts," she explained. "Then she was a writer, an author quite big in the Nineties."

Colin coughed under his breath and his shoulders sagged.

"I'm not sure we have a lot in common."

He looked at Eliza's straight shoulders longingly as she typed.

"Colin, she's been a touch-typist for years," Amy pointed out. "She still types address labels for her Christmas cards!"

Colin realised that Amy and Eliza had the same tinkling laugh.

"I think you'll have lots in common," Amy continued. "More than you know.

"This shop is full of stories about where typewriters have been and where they came from. You love all that.

"Gran has a lot of stories about her typewriters," Amy continued, "She may even recognise some in here; she probably used some of those models at work."

Colin shrugged off his fleecy jacket as if he had a sudden craving to live in a tropical country.

His eyes hadn't left Eliza's back.

"Can you mind the shop tomorrow, Amy?" he asked her. "I can invite Eliza for afternoon tea tomorrow?"

Amy left his side for a moment and moved closer to her gran.

Colin saw the likeness in them in the way they held themselves as if suspended by a coat hanger, an elegant padded one in a perfectly arranged, scented wardrobe.

Amy looked back at Colin and nodded to her gran, deep in conversation.

Eliza turned and looked over her shoulder; she had violet eyes, just like her typewriter ribbon.

When she smiled gently in agreement towards Colin, her face was a vase of the most beautiful scented pink roses.

Every typewriter in the shop wore a smile.

•   •   •   •

Colin stepped towards the door and lifted his face to the sun setting behind the tall Georgian buildings of Edinburgh's handsome New Town.

Inside the shop behind him, the light shone, yellow and inviting, with the sounds of the students drifting out to the street.

Above the sound of chat and laughter came the steady, clear strike of Eliza's perfect touch-typing that was music to his ears.

Colin turned to peer back into the shop.

It was four walls containing multiple stories old and new, with the latest yet to be typed up.

Colin had always loved old machinery and in particular typeset, print and typewriters.

Now he understood the real reason he opened the shop in the first place.

Even as he visualised their names, Colin and Eliza, in various fonts in a violet colour, he knew it wasn't just about the machinery.

It truly was about finding kindred spirits, finding his own story – their story – to be typed letter by letter, word by word.

She was as exotic to him as the Olivetti Valentine was in a row of jobbing type-writers.

He couldn't let this slip through his fingers.

"We're going down to the St Vincent Bar for drinks and supper, Colin. Join us!" Amy called with a reassuring smile.

He opened his mouth to decline, but she cut him off, raising a hand in front of him.

"Come on, Colin! It's your shop. Come and thank everyone."

"They don't even notice I'm here," he muttered sullenly as he looked achingly towards Eliza.

Amy followed his gaze.

"I'll make sure Gran comes?" she bribed.

"Ach, OK, then, Amy," he agreed. "I am grateful, really. I'm not sure I've sold any typewriters, though!"

"Well, not tonight . . . but just wait until these photos hit social media!

"I've popped up an Instagram story already. People are in love with it!"

She held out the screen of her mobile, and in front of him was a moody shot of the inside of the shop that scanned smoothly around the student group then came to a rest at the side of Eliza typing on the red Olivetti Valentine.

Her fingers were going in time to the music Amy had posted with the video.

It was truly magical.

"I'm not at all surprised that people are in love." He coughed. "I mean, you did a good job, Amy."

• • • •

They floated away in groups down the hill, further into the New Town, past the railed gardens and along cobbled roads, reaching the St Vincent Bar on the corner.

Straggling at the back after locking up were Colin, Amy and Eliza.

Eliza wore a long teddy fur coat, and at her side swung the red plastic bucket case of her Olivetti Valentine.

"You could have left it in the shop, you know," Colin told her.

"Oh, thanks, but I'm a little attached to it. It was my father's."

Colin's ears perked up. The typewriters with the nicest stories always sold best.

"You must tell me about him," Colin said enthusiastically.

It was easier to talk to Eliza through the medium of her typewriter, even if it was closed up for the evening in its red plastic case, which now sat at the side of their table as they waited for their round of drinks and snacks to appear.

"Tell us about my great-grandpa," Amy said to Eliza, who was in the middle of the group.

Eliza sighed.

"Who wants to know about an old newspaperman who worked in the noise of old typewriters, typeset and pounding presses right in the middle of Edinburgh?"

"We do!" the group chorused.

Colin sat up straight, giving his attention to Eliza, whose face was radiant in the soft glow of the pub.

"He was a newspaper man through and through," she began. "He bought this typewriter in 1971 after hearing about it on the radio.

"I was eight years old and I thought I'd never seen anything as delicious as this."

And when she lifted the case in the air, Colin felt a quickening of his breath as he'd seen nothing so delicious as this combination of woman and machine.

An animated Eliza continued with her story and the students were riveted.

"He worked in offices up on the North Bridge and I vividly remember visiting the reporters' room, the noise, the clatter and the cigarette smoke." She laughed. "That's where stories were generated."

Her head turned left and right and all attention was on her.

"But mind, this was in the days before delete, copy and paste!

"They turned stories into a form that others could read after they were set in metal rows.

"Typesetters clanked and clinked rows of letters into metal plates, while in a thunderous basement the machines rolled and pressed those happenings on to paper."

Everyone in their corner of the pub could visualise the former newspaper offices up on the North Bridge.

Journalists upstairs, typesetters downstairs and, under the bridge, tied bundles of newspapers being hurled into the back of vans for delivery throughout Edinburgh and to Waverley station to go beyond the city.

"Fascinating!" one of the young poets called out. "I say we toast your father, Eliza and your great-grandad, Amy. Here's to the newspaper man!"

Eliza closed her eyes momentarily.

"To Dad!" she whispered.

"He was an astute man to buy the Olivetti Valentine," Colin said as he sat next to Eliza, their hips touching.

"Oh, I don't think he was thinking about any future value," she admitted. "They had all kinds of typewriters in the office – a right mixture.

"He just thought that this one was something special at the time, and it does kind of scream the Seventies, doesn't it?"

"I guess it does, yes," he replied with a smile. "It was designed by Ettore Sottsass and launched on Valentine's Day in 1969."

As they spoke, Colin's eyes never left Eliza's.

The chatter of the students became mere background noise.

"You're sure you are OK with volunteering alongside Amy?" he continued, hoping so much that she would say yes.

"I said I would, didn't I?" she replied softly.

"Oh, yes, you did. I just wanted to make sure."

"You wanted to make sure that me and the Olivetti Valentine don't run out on you?" She laughed.

But then she saw Colin's face fall.

"I'm joking!" she quickly assured him.

Colin nodded.

"We should have held the Poets Night/Poets Type next week when it is actually Valentine's Day," he admitted.

"Perhaps Amy and her friends will be too busy that night to be bothered with a typewriter shop," Eliza replied.

Colin looked serious.

"Yes, of course," he said.

"But there's nothing stopping us doing a little something that day, too," Eliza added.

Then her face brightened.

"I have an idea that might need Amy and her mobile phone apps for those little films she does so well."

● ● ● ●

The following week, The Right Type had a special window display.

The red Olivetti Valentine stood centre stage amidst a carpet of red paper hearts.

From the carriage sprung a bouquet of red roses and a sign that said *Hearts For Sale* and red cardboard arrows pointed to Valentine's poems and cards available.

The other window showcased Colin's latest find: a white Olivetti Valentine.

It was surrounded by pots of white snowdrops that nodded each time the door to the shop opened.

Inside, Eliza served customers an array of Valentine's cards.

Colin was finding it hard to concentrate, as he'd discovered something in his own Olivetti Lettera 22 vintage typewriter that morning when he'd opened up shop.

I'm going on a trip to New York, the piece of red paper said, *where there are lots of typewriter shops.*

There's a copy of the Olivetti Valentine in the Museum of Modern Art if you'd like to join me. I've arranged volunteers for the shop.

It wasn't signed, but the A5 piece of red paper was typed up in violet-blue cursive script font.

Colin had never received a Valentine in his life, and this was by far the best he could ever receive.

He moved through the shop, humming as he slid typewriter carriages to their resting places, then typed a few lines on the Olivetti Lettera.

When Eliza was showing someone out of the shop, he picked a red rose from the window display to place beside a piece of red paper he placed on her table.

I most whole-heartedly accept your kind invitation. Love from your Valentine.

Colin moved to the door where Eliza stood, slipped his hand into hers and they stood contentedly under the sign: *The Right Type.* ▪

21

My Sunshine

BY LYNDA FRANKLIN

'M going now, Mum. Bye!"

"Wait a minute!"

Jen put down the carrot she was scraping and ran to the front door.

She was too late. The sound of the door slamming was already echoing up the hall.

It hung in the air for a few seconds before fading into nothing.

She sighed gently, wishing that she didn't feel this strange feeling of loss at being deprived of a proper goodbye.

He would be back in a few hours.

She took a deep breath. It was fine. He was sixteen after all, not six.

Only somehow it wasn't fine.

Jen had been sixteen once. Jen had been in the clutches of puberty and hormones and everything in between.

She hadn't slammed doors and not bothered to tell her mother where she was going.

She hadn't shrugged every time she was asked a question or rolled her eyes when asked to do something.

She hadn't taken her phone to the bathroom and spent hours sitting perched on the edge of the bath talking to goodness knows who.

OK, smartphones didn't exist back then, but that wasn't the point.

She'd had a time to be home by and friends who came to the house so her parents could meet them.

What had happened to the little boy with soft blond curls whose face lit up each time he saw her?

Her little sunshine. That's what she used to call him, gently crooning the song to him when he was little.

"You are my sunshine, my only sunshine. You make me happy when skies are grey."

He would snuggle his warm, little body into her and giggle.

As he got older, he would sigh but grin, and she knew he still loved to hear her sing their special song.

When did she last sing to him – even as a joke?

Jen knew his lovely hair would likely darken from silky blond to brown.

But she didn't expect the purple streaks to appear, which looked odd and came with a letter from his school tutor.

Their uniform policy did not support such hairstyles, it declared.

When she spoke to him about it, Jason gave one of his famous shrugs.

"He's jealous because he hasn't got much hair," he told her.

Illustration: Shutterstock.

Jason arrived home one day with one ear pierced.

It was small and gold, and Jen told herself it wasn't that bad.

He couldn't be bothered to take care of it and it became infected.

Eventually he took it out.

Jen said nothing. She wouldn't judge.

She wouldn't let him know how worried she was – how much she longed to pull him towards her in a bear hug.

This was a phase. Isn't that what everyone told her? Isn't that what her husband told her?

"I daresay I did some crazy things when I was young," he said. "It's part of growing up."

Maybe it was, but that didn't make it any better.

She missed the, easy-going boy who was happy to go to the supermarket with her or load the dishwasher without an argument.

He answered her when she spoke back then.

He shared what had happened during his day and occasionally asked about hers.

Homemade cards, flagging flowers, limp toast in bed. Those Mother's Days were the best.

She remembered Jason climbing into bed with her and watching intently as she forced down each cold Marmite soldier.

There was usually a cup of weak orange juice on the tray, half spilt and dripping on to the duvet.

And a card, sticky with crepe paper and glitter. She'd kept every one.

Had Jason even remembered it was Mother's Day this Sunday?

• • • •

It was seven a.m., and Jason was pouring cornflakes into a bowl while staring into his phone.

"Morning," Jen said cheerily. "It's a bit early for you, isn't it? Dad's not even up yet."

"I've got football practice in half an hour." He stuck his phone in his pocket and looked up. "We have an important game coming up."

"Oh, right." She made herself coffee and sat down. "You'll be home for lunch, won't you?

"It's roast beef – one of your favourites." She hesitated. "I thought I'd treat myself."

She immediately felt foolish at dropping such a stupid hint about the specialness of today.

"Yeah, I'll be back," Jason said. "Have you seen my knee pads?"

"They're in the cupboard under the sink."

He stuffed them into his rucksack.

"See you."

Jen wasn't sure what to say, but she needed to say something.

"Don't be late, will you," she murmured softly in the end.

Jason turned.

"I said I'd be back. I've got to go or I'll be late."

She heard the customary slam of the front door.

"Happy Mother's Day to me," Jen muttered, automatically picking up a yellow petal she could see on the floor.

She hadn't really expected anything, so why did she feel so disappointed?

She could see another petal lying outside the utility room and walked over to pick it up.

It was yellow like the other one.

She turned it over in her hand, wondering how it got there.

She opened the door.

A small bunch of sunflowers were propped up in the sink.

Next to them, on the draining board, she could see a card.

She stared at it for a second before quickly opening it.

Her heart skipped a beat as she looked at the big, hand-drawn sun on the page.

It was coloured thickly in yellow crayon with yellow lines pointing out in all directions.

It was the sort of sun everyone draws when they first learn to draw a sun – big and bright and bold.

She smiled, her eyes making it hard to make out the words at first.

Blinking the tears away, she read Jason's scrawling handwriting.

Thanks, Mum. Lots of love from your little sunshine!

Her phone suddenly buzzed with a message.

Forgot sorry. Happy Mum's Day. See u later. J x

Jen held the card against her. Her boy was growing up.

He was experimenting and trying new things – sometimes getting it right, sometimes wrong.

It was her job to be there and help him through these years, celebrating each small triumph with him and easing his way gently through the rough patches.

She picked up a vase and filled it with water, carefully arranging the sunflowers and smiling at the splash of sunshine they brought to her special day.

Very quietly she began to hum.

"You are my sunshine, my only sunshine.

"You make me happy when skies are grey . . ."

WINKIE THE PIGEON

DURING World War II, an RAF Beaufort bomber was shot down over the North Sea in 1942.

The crew, unable to communicate, sent their homing pigeon, Winkie, to their base near Dundee. Despite the 120-mile journey, Winkie arrived exhausted but safe.

By calculating the time difference between the plane's last known location and Winkie's arrival, the RAF estimated the crash site. A rescue mission was launched and the crew were found and rescued within 15 minutes.

Winkie's heroic flight saved the lives of the airmen.

Winkie the pigeon was stuffed after she passed away and is on display in Dundee's McManus art gallery and museum.

Image: Shutterstock.

A Drop Of Hope

BY EIRIN THOMPSON

JEAN and I had spent the morning visiting Jean's old friend, Judy, from her days working in the bank.

Judy was in her seventies, like us, and had lost her husband almost a year earlier.

"It's not so much that I miss having a husband," Judy had explained to us over coffee and cake. "It's that I miss John very specifically."

I'd nodded.

Even though I'd been a widow for long enough to get over the initial shock and the period of readjustment, I still had moments of yearning for a simple hug from Dennis, with that way he had of locking his fingers behind the small of my back.

I missed his smile, his dry wit, his can-do attitude to life.

Like Judy, I didn't miss having a husband in a general sense; I didn't miss the mere idea of it.

But oh, at moments I still missed my Dennis keenly.

Luckily for me, fate had given me Jean – a friend beyond compare.

And there we sat, admiring Judy's coffee mugs and commenting appreciatively on her cake, which she happily admitted was shop-bought.

"What do you have planned for this afternoon, Judy?" Jean enquired.

"Father Brown and a little cross-stitch," Judy replied. "How about you?"

"We're heading up to Crockard Hall to do their Snowdrop Walk," I answered.

"How lovely!" Judy exclaimed. "I hope it's wonderful."

"Why don't you come with us?" I suggested. "Can Father Brown and your cross-stitching wait until tomorrow?"

Judy sighed.

"It's very nice of you to offer, but I'm afraid I can't walk far these days," she admitted. "I'm all right knocking about the house, and I can take a stroll through town, if I plan my route according to where there are benches.

"As for setting out for a proper walk – I'm afraid that's a non-starter."

"I'm sorry to hear that," Jean

Illustration: Ruth Blair.

replied. "It must be frustrating for you."

"I've decided not to mind," Judy replied. "If I started feeling sorry for myself, I'd just end up miserable.

"No, as far as I'm concerned," she added, "I'm going to count my blessings. I can still go shopping with a bit of forethought, and I have daughters and grandchildren who drive. They take me here and there."

Soon, Jean and I hit the road.

Crockard Hall isn't exactly a stately home, but it is a very grand old manor house that is now looked after by a trust.

You can take a tour of the interior during the summer months and at Christmas, led by volunteers.

The grounds are open in every season, and there is always something to see.

Jean parked her car on the crunchy gravel and we changed from our shoes into our wellington boots.

"The Snowdrop Walk starts on Ladies' Mile," I told Jean. "I read about it in the newspaper the other day."

"Oh, lovely – that's a lovely spot for a stroll at any time,"

➤ Jean commented.

We set off round the corner behind the hall and there it was: wow!

A dense carpet of milky white snowdrops lined both sides of the footpath for as far as the eye could see.

"It's spell-binding!" Jean exclaimed with a gasp.

"I wish I could paint it in a picture," I replied. "But I can't draw for toffee.

"And anyway, how would you capture this?" I pointed out. "Surely you have to see it for yourself."

Jean dug out her phone and took a few snaps.

"I'd like to show Judy," she explained, "though photos won't do it justice."

"That's a nice idea."

We walked the length of Ladies' Mile, then followed the snowdrop-lined path along the riverbank, through a wood and back towards the hall.

My Mother's Patchwork Bag

My mother has a patchwork bag, its colours bright and bold;
The bits and pieces of her life are the stories it has told.
A patterned piece with roses and this patch of vivid lime
Are from my grandma's aprons; she wore them all the time.
I remember Grandma, white hair and smiley face.
She bought us books and taught us to always know our place.

Here's a piece of yellow and a square of black and tan –
They're from my grandpa's waistcoats, a lively, dapper man.
This crumpled patch of khaki is what my father wore;
It reminds us of his comrades and the awful things they saw.
Here's a piece that's special – I know you'll never guess –
This piece of oyster satin is from my wedding dress.

There's a swathe of orange, and a flash of crimson, too,
Some psychedelic colours that clash with every hue.
She wore them in the Sixties, with floral trouser suits

"We're almost back at the start," I told Jean. "But I don't want to leave just yet.

"Shall we sit on this bench and just enjoy the vista for a while?" I suggested.

We plonked ourselves down and gazed at the snowdrops.

"Each one of them is only little. Tiny, really," Jean observed. "Yet when you see them all together, they're magnificent.

"It's such a pity that Judy couldn't join us."

"We're very lucky, you know," I replied. "It's so easy to take it for granted that we're still fully mobile.

"It isn't until you meet someone who isn't that you realise what you've got."

"Agreed." Jean nodded. "I love the fact that you and I can jump in the car and have a little outing like this, or stroll round the lake in the park.

"We can go for a ramble or even a hike any time we like."

Or sometimes with a mini and her thigh-high leather boots.
The boys wore velvet jackets, boot-lace ties and slicked-back hair –
Look at my mother's patchwork and you can see them there.

There's a splash of navy from a fireman's uniform,
And from my daughter's party dress a rainbow unicorn.
A piece of shiny silver from the costume of a clown
And a fragment I remember from my graduation gown.
Every patch was stitched with love, some are stained with tears
Every one a memory, garnered over years

I wouldn't swap my mother's bag for a Mulberry made of gold,
For my mother's precious memories are the treasures it can hold.
A mosaic of her memories, of things she held so dear,
Of people past and gone away, to keep them ever near.
In future years when work is done and my chicks have flown,
I think I'll sew a patchwork bag with memories of my own.

Kay Seeley

Illustration by Shutterstock.

"To be fair, we've never actually hiked."

"Maybe not, but we could, if we wanted to," Jean pointed out. "And maybe we should, while we still can. You never know what's round the corner, Maureen."

I nodded.

"Ready for home?" Jean asked.

"Sure."

We took the path that led through the cobbled courtyard, where we came on a stall offering clumps of snowdrops to take home and plant for a voluntary donation.

"Hey, Maureen!" Jean cried. "Look at this! We can get some snowdrops to bring to Judy.

"I know, we could wait until she goes out and plant them in her garden, where she can see them from the window, and put a little note through her door."

The kindness of taking the spring flowers to Judy was very Jean, and so was the little dramatic twist of making them into a surprise.

"OK," I agreed with a smile. "Let's do it."

Before we left Crockard Hall, we found a different bench and sat down for one last view of the snowdrop carpet.

"By the way," Jean began. "Why is Ladies' Mile so-called, do you think?"

"Oh, I don't know," I admitted. "Do you want me to Google it?"

I took out my phone.

"I can't find anything about country houses, but it says here that Ladies' Mile was a commercial retail centre for New York folk from the mid to late 1800s, and into the twentieth century. Apparently it got its name because of the fashionable department stores.

"The area became so popular with female shoppers that it meant women felt safe going there to do their shopping unaccompanied by men," I finished.

"New York, New York. So good they named it twice, Maureen," Jean replied. "Poor old Judy has to make a strategic plan just to go into town, and here we are able to do what we like and not even using that ability."

"Are you saying we should go on another holiday, Jean?" I asked.

"I'm saying it does seem a pity to squander all this good health by not going."

"I'd need to renew my passport," I told her.

Jean turned to me with a gleeful face.

"Then you're up for it?"

"Like you say, it would be a pity not to."

I imagined Dennis overhearing our conversation and grinning.

He wouldn't have wanted my life to stop when he passed away. And he would have loved Jean, too, although possibly in small doses.

As I mentioned, Dennis met life with a can-do approach, and I knew he would have told me to travel the world if I fancied it.

"Let's take lots of trips in the future," I told Jean. "Every day is precious and we need to make them count."

Jean jumped up, threw her arms around me and squeezed.

It wasn't a Dennis hug, but it was very nice.

BEAULIEU RIVER, HAMPSHIRE

BEAULIEU, a historic estate in the heart of the New Forest, offers not only history and nature, but a fascinating slice of automotive heritage. Palace House, the ancestral home of the Montagu family, has been open to the public since 1952. The adjacent National Motor Museum houses a world-class collection of vehicles, from vintage classics to modern marvels.

Visitors can explore the beautiful grounds, including the tranquil Beaulieu Abbey and the enchanting Alice's Adventures in Wonderland topiary garden. The estate also offers opportunities for outdoor activities, such as walking, cycling and boating on the Beaulieu River.

For those interested in maritime history, Buckler's Hard, a historic shipbuilding yard nearby, is a must-see. Here, visitors can learn about the construction of Nelson's Navy and explore the charming village setting.

Homeward Bound

BY GABRIELLE MULLARKEY

WHEN she'd booked her passage home, Lorna had initially overlooked the fact that her visit would coincide with Easter.

She had been more concerned with ensuring she got a good travel deal.

Besides, the trip had taken not only a chunk of her savings, but a lot of her resolve.

Like most emigrants, a longing to go home was mixed with trepidation and self-doubt about stepping back into a world left behind.

Would she have changed too much to slip back, temporarily, into her old life?

And did she even want to?

Her parents, of course, were beside themselves with excitement.

It was five years since they'd waved her off at Cobh on a sea crossing to New York – and now here she was, returning by aeroplane, no less!

She emerged into a cool, cloudy day outside Shannon Airport to find her dad, John, waiting.

They embraced in silence. Both had shining eyes when they parted.

"You flew," he said, taking her suitcase and putting it in the back of his spluttery old truck. "What does home look like from up there?"

"I didn't get a chance to see much as we left because of cloud cover," she replied, before realising he'd meant what did Ireland look like, not New York.

"As we came in to land, the fields looked like a hand-stitched quilt in green," she amended, sliding into the passenger side of the truck. "Not quite forty shades, but not far off."

This was a fib, as the cloud cover had been thick here, too.

Still, her father's look of delight was enough to convince her it was a harmless fib.

He gazed at her woollen yellow coat.

"You'd no need to dress up on our account. I see you've a new suitcase as well," he added, nodding towards the back of the truck.

She was about to point out that the old thing she left with was falling to bits even then, when she realised how that would sound.

The pale-blue cardboard valise she'd left with five years earlier

Illustration: Pat Gregory.

had been given to her by her mother as if she was handing over an ancient treasure.

"How is everyone, Da?" she asked instead. "Mam and Aunt Monica? And you?"

"Oh, we're ticking over nicely," he replied. "If we'd any major news, it would have been in our letters."

She dipped her head to hide her blushes. She didn't always put her major news in airmail letters. Some things had to be said face to face.

"And you coming back for Easter once you'd saved up enough!" Her dad sighed blithely as he pulled away from the airport. "We knew you wouldn't forget that it's your mam and aunt's favourite time of year – despite the weather.

"That's why Mam didn't come to the airport. She's giving the house its Easter clean."

"Oh, yes."

"On Easter Sunday there's Mass in the morning and then a visit to the well." He paused. "And in the afternoon, the cake dance.

"I bet they won't have seen the like of that in New York!" he added triumphantly.

"No," she agreed, "though there are other dances to attend, if you so wish."

A tea dance was how her parents had met.

"You'll be taking part in the cake dance, I dare say," her father went on. "You always could cut a rug.

"Your mam's been talking you up to everyone in Carraig Dearg, you know." He paused again. "She's hoping you'll dance with Sean, no doubt."

Lorna chose to look out of the window as the County Clare countryside rolled by.

There was a line she'd read by a poet recently that said that the best poetry was about "making the familiar strange".

She understood that better now.

After five years away, everything about home was at once achingly familiar yet somehow mysterious.

She wondered if you changed to fit into the landscape around you, or if you were changed by it.

After five years away she was no closer to solving the mystery.

"Will you be an object of curiosity as a returnee?" Vic had asked her before she left, watching her fold clothes into her new suitcase.

"Of course not," she'd claimed.

She'd met many New Yorkers – especially true locals, such as Vic – who thought she must be either pining for home or never looking back.

The truth was somewhere in between.

And now here she was, in her father's truck, turning off the road past the old Famine graveyard and up the track to the farm. Her real home.

Her mother, Eileen, was standing on the stoop of the back door, waiting.

They embraced for a long moment, during which neither felt any inclination to disentangle.

"I hope you didn't spend a fortune getting here," Eileen said briskly as she led Lorna into the house, her dad coming in behind with the suitcase.

Lorna admitted to buying a ticket for $260.

"That's a good deal," she told her mother on seeing her suck in her breath.

"I'm earning good money now," she added defensively.

She was a book-keeper for a tailor on the Lower East Side and shared a house with three other women – Italian and Mexican – in the Bowery.

Inside the house, Lorna had to get her bearings once again.

The marble-effect clock still ticked over the kitchen mantel.

The couch was still draped with crocheted antimacassars.

She felt a lump in her throat, which thickened when Aunt Monica hobbled into the room on her stick.

"I thought I heard an American twang there."

Aunt Monica grinned as Lorna rushed over to embrace her and guide her into an armchair.

"You shouldn't be on your feet," Eileen warned her.

"Oh, my feet will forget what they're for soon." Aunt Monica snorted. "Let me look at you, Lorna. I hear you're taking evening classes in accounts.

"That's good, that's very good. It's important to get on."

Lorna nodded, even though exhaustion was setting in.

"Let the girl get in the door before we start asking all sorts,"

John said, handing Lorna her case. "I expect you can find your own way to your room. It hasn't upped and moved!"

Nodding and smiling, she went upstairs with her case, grateful for the chance to gather her thoughts for a few moments alone.

Her parents looked well, though, as did Aunt Monica.

Although Monica was only six years older than her sister, she'd had a hard life, effectively raising Eileen and her three other siblings when their parents died.

She'd eventually become a librarian in a nearby town, only to be badly affected by arthritis in her forties.

When it was too difficult for her to cope alone, she'd moved in with Eileen and John.

Lorna had been nine or ten at the time.

She never recalled Aunt Monica complaining or feeling sorry for herself, not even at having to give up her beloved dancing.

Year in, year out as a young woman she had been crowned Queen of the Feast at the Easter cake dance after dancing with whichever nimble-footed companion could keep up with her.

Then it had been Lorna's turn to pick up the baton and continue a proud family tradition.

The dance took place, rain or shine, in the village square on Easter Sunday afternoon and anyone who wished could dance to the tunes of Tadhg Higgins, a talented local piper.

It was traditional for the men and women, boys and girls to take part first in a group dance, then gradually split off into pairs for a waltz or an energetic jig, depending on age.

For the three years before she emigrated, Lorna had danced with Sean Butler, the son of the local tobacconist.

They had twice been awarded the cake as "the best and sprightliest dancers".

In actual fact, the cake was a barmbrack specially spiced and baked for the occasion.

It was not something she had explained to Vic or anyone else she'd met in New York.

Now she wasn't certain why. Was it because she wanted to treasure the memory of the tradition? Or had she been shy of mentioning Sean, especially to Vic?

But that was daft. She and Sean might have had an understanding years ago their teens, but by the time she left home at the age of twenty-five they'd moved into an acceptance of friendship.

She unpacked and went down to the kitchen for a cuppa with a slice of barmbrack.

"Now, your mum wants you to taste that on account of a singular honour she's been awarded this year," her dad said with a twinkle in his eye. "She's making the one for the cake dance."

Eileen blushed with pride and pleasure as Lorna bit into the curranty richness of the brack.

"It's delicious," Lorna confirmed, sipping the wonderful accompanying tea. "But you have made brack for the cake dance before, Mam."

"Yes, but you're home for it," Eileen explained. "That makes it special."

There was a tap on the door.

"Knock, knock." Sean's voice carried through the house. "I smelled the brack a good mile off and followed it all the way here."

He stepped in, grinning.

"I was keen to see the traveller returned, of course. How are you, Lorna?"

• • • •

Half an hour later, Lorna joined Sean on a walk past the Famine graveyard and up to the little chapel built by past emigrants in tribute to their ancestors.

Despite the cool day, they sat on a low wall near the church, the slope in front of them bathed in a patch of sudden sunshine.

"You're wearing trousers," he noted.

"Does that scandalise you?"

He laughed heartily, throwing back his fine head of dark hair.

"I'm only teasing," she admitted with a smile, finding his laugh infectious.

"I was thinking of my mam's sister," he told her. "My aunt Celia. Three years ago she came over from America to visit my grandfather. Six weeks on a steamer, two buses and a taxi ride to reach his front door.

"And what does Grandad say to her when he opens it? 'Come back when you're dressed decently!'"

He shook his head.

"He wouldn't let her in because she was wearing trousers!"

Lorna folded her arms.

"I hope she forced her way in and told him not to be so daft."

"I'm sure she did, knowing Aunt Celia." Sean grinned. "I've only got my mam's word for the story, though.

"When Aunt Celia did go back to America, I wonder if she said, 'never again'."

He sneaked a look at Lorna.

"I hope you won't be saying 'never again' once you leave after this visit."

"Give me a chance, I've only just got here!"

"Will you be doing all the usual for Easter?" he asked.

Lorna scuffed her boots in the soil at her feet.

"Yep. Mass on Easter Sunday morning, then to the well for drawing the water and the cake dance in the afternoon."

The drawing of the water from the healing well was a tradition as old as the cake dance, with origins just as shrouded in myth.

The well lay on the edge of the village. Every villager filled a cup from the bucketfuls of water winched up, then scattered it on whoever needed healing – Eileen scattered her cupful on Monica's hands and feet.

It wasn't as if anyone expected magical healing to occur – it was about respecting the past.

Same with the cake dance.

Lorna turned to him.

"I'm engaged, Sean. Back in New York. I haven't told my parents. Yet."

"Ah." He searched her face. "Let me guess. You don't want to kill off their lingering hope that you'll return for good, settle down with a local lad and forget all this gallivanting nonsense!"

She smiled wistfully.

"The farm is already promised to my cousin, Daragh, when Dad – you know – retires."

She cleared her throat as she said this, knowing her father would never retire.

36

The farm would pass out of his work-roughened, capable hands only on his deathbed.

"But that's not the reason you left in the first place," Sean pointed out gently. "Was it?"

"Oh, Sean, it had nothing to do with you!" she exclaimed with firm conviction.

She bit her lip and nodded out at the graveyard.

"In front of us is the past – all that struggle and hardship."

Then she turned to acknowledge the chapel.

"And behind us is the past in a different way: a stone tribute to the people buried in front of us, built by the people who survived by fleeing.

"I didn't join that particular exodus, Sean, but I did have plans that were too . . ."

"Too big for Carraig Dearg?" he prompted. "I won't be offended if you say it."

"It's not that. It's just, we're still finding our feet as a country – women, especially.

"I wanted more opportunity. I'm hoping to be an accountant, and the place where I'm working now as a book-keeper will pay for my training.

"In all honesty, I hadn't ruled out a return home with those qualifications under my belt until I met Vic."

"The fella you're engaged to?" Sean checked. "I know I'm not the reason you left, Lorna. I'm not daft enough to think we ever had more than a solid friendship. I wouldn't want to lose that for anything.

"But tell me: am I correct in thinking that Vic's not an Irish name?"

Lorna's lips curved upwards.

It was a relief to talk in the brisk air with someone of her own age about the best thing that had ever happened to her. Meeting Vic.

"His grandparents were Lithuanian Jews," she told him. "I met him when I got knocked to my feet one morning on my way to work.

"A guy came running out of a store after robbing it, bumped into me and sent me flying.

"Not Vic!" she added, seeing Sean's face. "By knocking me over, the thief lost his turn of speed, allowing a couple of nearby cops to give chase and nab him. One of them was Vic."

"Now I've heard it all." Sean sighed, shaking his head. "Only you could meet the only cop in New York cop who's not Irish!"

She laughed. It felt good to laugh.

Until she remembered she'd yet to tell her parents she was engaged to a man from a different religion and culture.

Sean interpreted her expression.

"I shouldn't have told you that story about my grandad," he said. "Aunt Celia may have exaggerated it. She lives in Texas, where everything's this big . . ."

He demonstrated with his hands.

"Including the tall tales, I'm guessing." He grew serious. "You're right about a lot of things, Lorna. But we're a young country with high hopes. My da says we're about to be admitted to the United Nations.

"If that happens, I expect to be in New York myself for the after-party, and I hope you'll put ➤

me up!"

"Any time." She laughed, before growing anxious. "You won't mention what I told you about Vic, will you? I want to tell Mam and Dad first."

"On one condition," he replied, giving a wry smile. "That you give me a twirl or two at the cake dance."

"That should set tongues wagging." She rolled her eyes.

"Now, you need to get over yourself," Sean said gravely, but with a twinkle in his eye. "I think you'll find it'll be more a case of 'Lorna who?' when you go quickstepping across the village square.

"You're probably a rusty dancer anyway." He shrugged. "Tripping over that policeman's big feet."

She swatted him playfully and he rose to escort her home.

• • • •

By the time Easter Sunday arrived, Lorna felt more relaxed, but she hadn't yet told her family about Vic.

It was damp and breezy, but the good folk of Carraig Dearg were used to it.

By afternoon, the village was ready for the cake dance.

A large awning had been raised over the village square to keep the pitter-patter of April rain off.

Eileen's barmbrack was set up on a table in the centre. Everyone arriving went to admire it.

Then, one by one, local children placed a painted, hard-boiled egg around the cake in a decorative garland.

As far as Lorna was aware, each village and even different parts of the country had their own cake dance traditions.

Today, as usual, the dancers would have to navigate the table without jogging or dislodging the cake and delicately painted eggs – no-one wanted to send them flying!

Soon, most of the village seemed to be present, with those not dancing occupying cushion-covered benches just off the square.

Once the cake had been admired by all, a muslin cloth was draped over it.

As piper Tadhg flexed his elbow to pour out jigs, reels and planxties, Lorna followed the loose pattern of joining in when the mood took.

Then came the waltzes.

Lorna stepped to one side as her parents came together for a nifty performance, watched from the sidelines by a smiling Aunt Monica.

Lorna went to sit with her for a bit.

"I'm sorry you can't do this any more."

Monica touched her wrist.

"Don't tell your mam, but watching all the young folks shake a leg does me a power of good compared to the well water!"

As the waltzers twirled past the cake, Lorna met Sean's eye across the square.

They found a gap to come together and join in.

Lorna thought she might have forgotten the steps, but muscle memory kicked in.

As Sean twirled her, she caught sight of Aunt Monica smiling from the bench, cane gripped between her bunched knuckles.

The waltz ended, she thanked Sean and went back to join her aunt.

"Don't read anything into that, Auntie!" Lorna panted. "Just two old friends letting their feet do the talking."

Her aunt nodded, tapping her ankles up and down.

"Don't worry. I knew you and Sean were over before you ever began. You're meant for someone else, I think.

"Someone we haven't met yet," she added with a wink.

Lorna tuned to look at her aunt's twinkling eyes, which were far too perceptive, and blushed.

Luckily, at that moment, the piper stopped and called over to Monica.

"As a quickstepper of many a year, who do you choose to win the cake, Monica Brennan?"

Monica smiled and tapped her cane in the direction of a young couple, who squealed with delight.

The young man duly picked up the cake and handed it to his partner.

Then they both carried it over to Monica in its linen cloth and presented it to her as Queen of the Feast.

"None of that now." Monica laughed. "You two won fair and square. "Take it home to your mam's and dad's and enjoy a slice tonight."

As they skipped away, Monica whispered to Lorna.

"When I was a girl, the cake would be a huge thing and divided up amongst all attending. Ah, well."

She looked out across the square.

"Times change and we all move with them. Don't we, my dear?"

● ● ● ●

Lorna told her parents that night as they sat down to their Easter roast.

She produced a photo from her wallet of Vic in uniform.

"A fine-looking fella," her father said approvingly.

'I knew a Vic once from Trim," Eileen said, brows quirking as she added, "I'm guessing he's not from Trim?"

It was going to be all right, Lorna soon realised. All of it.

Her parents' only sadness was that she'd leave these shores in a few days and they might not meet again for many a day.

That thought brought a lump to her throat.

Until she thought of sitting with Sean at the old Famine chapel, talking about the past in front of her and the past behind her.

She told them all about Vic, then ran up to her room to fetch down what he'd given to her before she flew home.

"Not an engagement ring – we haven't chosen one yet," she murmured as she opened the little box. "It's not expensive or anything, but he thought I might like it as a reminder of where I'm from, once I told him what Carraig Dearg means in English."

It was a bracelet in the shape of a torc with a red stone set in the centre.

In English, Carraig Dearg could be translated as "red rock".

"I would have put it on first thing this morning," Lorna admitted. "Only I knew you'd wonder where it came from and I wanted to build up to my news."

Her parents looked at each other.

"And will you come back here to be married from St Finnian's?" her father asked delicately.

"We haven't thought that far yet," she admitted.

It was the most diplomatic way she could find to say, "neither of us are very religious."

Then she had a daring thought.

"If I got wed over there, perhaps you'd all come over? It would be . . . a trip home for both of you in a way."

Her parents looked at each other again.

"We'd like that, love." Eileen smiled. "When the time comes."

Eileen and John had emigrated separately to New York as youngsters – Eileen carrying her hopes in a brand-new, pale-blue cardboard valise.

Although she and John had known each other only vaguely before they left, they had only met properly at a tea dance run by one of the city's many Irish clubs.

And there they might have stayed, if John's father hadn't taken ill and his brother, in line to inherit the farm, announced that he was emigrating to London instead.

It turned out that John did want to run the family farm – something he'd never expected to come his way.

But he'd only return, he said, if it sat well with his fiancée.

So back home he and Eileen came after several years away, exchanging urban hustle and bustle, with all its opportunities and challenges, for the rural village life they'd thought lost to them forever rather than abandoned.

When Lorna had first talked of leaving, she'd asked her mother if she had any regrets about what she'd given up.

"We both have," Eileen had replied, to Lorna's surprise.

She'd assumed her father had never looked back over his shoulder.

"But you can't make any choice without regretting the road not taken," her mum had added. "The trick is to live with regrets but not be ruled by them."

And now Lorna knew that she must do the sam.

Her heart would be seared with homesick longing as she looked down at the green-stitched fields for the last time before clouds swallowed them up.

But she knew also that her heart would lift when those same clouds parted hours later to reveal glass and steel and the beating heart of a city where the man she loved was waiting for her.

"Count me out of going that far." Monica sighed, admiring the bracelet. "The way I see it, missy, is that fella of yours will have to get himself over here and be properly inspected. And the sooner the better."

"I'll think about it." Lorna grinned, loving them all.

She was already, in a way, missing them all, too.

But she would carry them with her – the way people she'd heard about carried a little bottle of earth from home – wherever she went. ◼

STREET CAT BOB

IN 2007, a ginger cat named Bob was found injured and alone in Islington. Rescued by homeless street vendor James Bowen, Bob became a beloved companion and a local celebrity, loved by everyone in the area.

The pair would busk together in London, with Bob often sporting a hand-knitted scarf.

Bob's heartwarming story, chronicled in James's bestselling books and a popular film released in 2016, captured the hearts of many.

To honor his legacy, a life-sized bronze statue of Bob, perched on books and wearing his signature scarf, was erected at Islington Green in 2021.

Image: Shutterstock.

Operation Spring Clean

BY ANNE PACK

GEORGE!"

"Oh, dear. I don't like the sound of that," George muttered from the comfort of his armchair.

He folded the newspaper he'd been reading and joined his wife in the hall.

"I can tell you're about to ask me to do something."

"Actually, *we* are going to do something," she replied.

"What's that?" George asked, suspicion in his voice.

"Clear out the loft."

George groaned.

"Now, before you say anything, we've been putting this off for longer than I care to remember," Carol told him firmly. "This year I am determined to complete Operation Spring Clean."

"But, Carol, it's the summer now, and I spent the entire day yesterday tidying out my shed, just like you asked me to," George reminded her.

"It was a lovely sunny day," she replied. "It was perfect for spreading everything out on the patio and getting rid of the things you no longer need or use."

George looked sheepish.

"That's the thing. I didn't get rid of anything – I put it all back again, because I need it all."

Carol raised an eyebrow and stood with her hands on her hips, waiting for an explanation.

"At least it's nice and tidy now and I know where everything is," he told her. "Anyway, I was hoping we could go to the garden centre today, have a cuppa and scone in the café and afterwards buy some bedding plants to cheer up the borders."

"Nice try, George." Carol looked up at the wall clock. "We've got the family coming round for a meal tonight, as you know. I've prepared everything. It all just needs to go in the oven.

"We have a window of a few hours during which we can do some de-cluttering."

She sighed.

"In a few years we'll be too old to get up there, and I don't want to leave all that for the family to do . . . eventually."

"But –"

"No more buts, George," Carol warned her husband. "You refused to do it last summer because you said it would be stifling hot.

"Then you wouldn't do it in the winter because you said it would

Illustration: Shutterstock.

be bitterly cold. It's perfect weather today."

George knew when he was beaten and obligingly opened the loft hatch and pulled down the ladder.

"Right," Carol said, putting her foot on the first rung. "The quicker we get started . . ."

There was a light switch just inside the hatch that George had installed shortly after they'd moved in as newlyweds almost 50 years ago.

He'd also floored the entire area and built some inexpensive flat pack bookcases for storage.

That was part of the problem.

They didn't know it at the time, but they were both unwilling to throw anything out in case it might have another use in the future.

George, being a joiner, created the perfect setting for squirrelling things away.

Over the years they did just that.

By the time their second daughter had outgrown her cot, it was dismantled and consigned to the loft, in safe storage until such times as they had grandchildren.

But by that time regulations had changed, and their daughters would not allow it to be used for their offspring, saying it was

> unsafe now.

It was a bitter blow, softened only by the fact they'd agreed to use the sleek pram that Carol insisted on having for her babies, and which they had lovingly kept.

Their grandsons had long since outgrown that, too, and it was safely packed away once again.

George had reluctantly skipped the cot, but he kept the wire base for drying his onions.

"It's like Aladdin's cave," George said in wonderment when his eyes had adjusted to the light.

Carol's heart sank. It was even worse than she'd remembered.

"If only there was a genie to magic it all away." She sighed.

"Oh, look! My old golf clubs."

With that, George was off to the far end of the loft to reminisce about his first set, which he'd built up as he could afford it.

These days he had top quality clubs that he used every week without fail.

But, like everything else, he couldn't bear to part with the old ones.

Carol shook her head and opened the nearest box.

It contained her late parents' wedding china, each piece individually encased in tissue paper.

She unwrapped a teacup and turned the delicate piece over in her hands, the forget-me-nots as vibrant as the day they were hand-painted.

The set had taken pride of place in the walnut display cabinet during Carol's childhood, but she couldn't recall it ever being used.

Meanwhile, George had discovered a lava lamp from the 1970s, declaring all it needed was a plug to bring it back to life.

After a couple of hours, progress was painfully slow.

They'd unearthed all manner of toys and games. They'd opened trunks full of woollen blankets and garish curtains.

They found a standard lamp with fringed shade and camping gear from holidays they'd had years ago.

There was an empty tropical fish tank and a budgie's cage.

Carol could have wept with the enormity of the task, and George was little help.

He was like a child in a sweet shop.

They should have cleared it out years ago. She knew that now.

A noise downstairs broke into her thoughts, and a few moments later a head popped up through the hatch.

It was their eldest daughter, Hannah.

"What are you two up to?" Hannah climbed up into the loft. "I haven't been up here in years. Wow."

Carol stood up from where she'd been sitting rummaging through a box of costume jewellery she'd forgotten she had.

"Hello, love." Carol rubbed her lower back to ease the stiffness. "In case you hadn't guessed, we're attempting to have a clear-out. Time must have run away with us."

"We're early," Hannah replied. "Rory's football match was cancelled so we thought we'd come over. I don't envy you your task. Can we help?"

Something caught Hannah's eye.

"Well, I never. Is that my doll's

house?"

"Don't you start." Carol chuckled. "Your dad's treating everything like long-lost treasure. We're supposed to be throwing things out."

"You can't throw out my doll's house!" Hannah got down on her knees to inspect it, and Carol rolled her eyes. "It's so much smaller than I remember."

She opened the front and gasped.

"You kept all the furniture."

"We keep everything." George laughed. "Or hadn't you noticed."

"Feel free to take it," Carol said only half joking.

"Too right I will. The school nursery will bite my hand off for this. What else have you got?"

Their son-in-law, Ben, joined them, along with Rory and his younger brother, Jack.

Boxes were feverishly opened and contents examined.

By the time Hannah's sister, Wendy, arrived with her crew, Hannah had laid claim to much of the toys for the nursery where she worked.

The loft by now was a bit crowded, so Carol excused herself to the kitchen.

She was pleased with the space they'd gained, but there was still a long way to go.

Over dinner, even the grandchildren were reliving the fun they'd had with the wooden fort complete with drawbridge that George had made for them.

"Do you have any plans for the rest of the stuff?" Wendy asked, helping herself to another roast potato.

"I'm minded to hire a skip or two and throw the lot in it,"

Carol admitted.

She wasn't joking. She wasn't sure her aching joints could stand days on end going through stuff.

This was met by loud protests.

"We'll get there," George added, patting Carol's hand. "A little at a time."

Carol slapped her hand on the table a little harder than she'd intended.

"We've been here before, George," she snapped. "This year I am determined to have an empty loft. One way or another."

"We're partly to blame." Wendy looked at her husband, Rob. "When we moved house we boxed things up, put it in your loft and never reclaimed it.

"Look, I'm free most of next weekend. I'll come over and help to categorise things. It's the least we can do."

She appealed round the table for volunteers.

"Count us in," Hannah added, with full agreement from her family.

"If you want, I can photograph things and advertise them on the community website," Rory offered, holding his phone aloft.

"Oh, I don't know. Some of it isn't worth anything." Carol frowned.

"For those items we can add 'free to a good home'." Hannah suggested.

"One person's junk is another's treasure," Ben added sagely.

Everything else can be offered to charity. Some of them do pick-ups, you know," Rob said.

For the first time that day, Carol could feel the strain and stress of what earlier had seemed like a gargantuan task disappear, just like the food her grandsons were vacuuming up in front of her.

She took a leisurely sip of wine and relaxed into her seat.

"Sounds like a plan."

"Our old lava lamp should fetch a good price, for starters." George raised his glass. "It's probably a collector's item by now."

Carol scoffed.

"A collector's item? More like it should be in a museum."

"They've become quite popular again," Wendy replied. "It'll sell really quickly, especially since it's vintage."

"Popular? Vintage?"

George's brows came together, and he looked across at Carol.

"Maybe we should hang on to it . . ."

"George!"

A Day Out In London

It's years since I have been here
And, at first, it feels quite strange
To see the difference time has made,
Though some things never change.

And that is what I focus on
Whilst I walk where famous feet
Have gone before, as Blue Plaques show
On buildings in each street.

I take in all the landmarks:
Saint Paul's, Trafalgar Square,
The Kings Road, where new fashion trends
Were soon sold everywhere.

I worked in London long ago
And was, at first, enchanted,
But with the routine and commute
I soon took it all for granted.

As I head now for the station,
Passing through St James's Park,
I can feel that energy coming back
As the city leaves its mark.

John Darley

Illustration: Shutterstock.

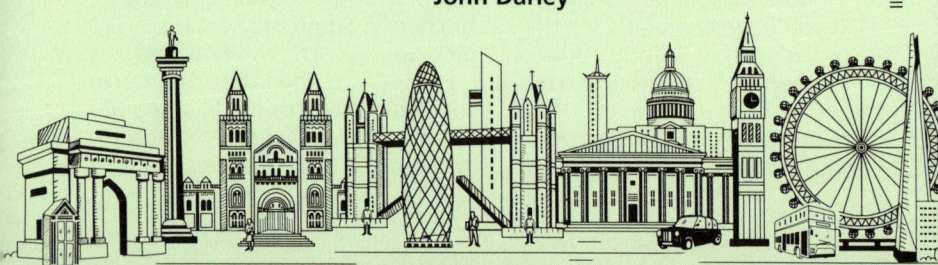

INVERBERVIE, ABERDEENSHIRE

THE coastal town of Inverbervie, or "Bervie" as the locals call it, sits on the edge of the North Sea. Its royal status stems from a visit by King David II in 1341. A pleasant coastal walk leads from Inverbervie to the historic fishing ports of Gourdon and Johnshaven. The route follows the former railway line, offering stunning views of the North Sea.

Gourdon, known locally as "Gurden", is a picturesque fishing village with a working harbour. Visitors can explore the Maggie Law Maritime Museum, which showcases the town's maritime heritage.

Johnshaven, another historic fishing port, boasts a beautiful harbour and stunning coastal scenery. The town's history is intertwined with the fishing industry and visitors can still witness the traditional way of life.

Dress The Part

BY SARA PARTINGTON

WHERE have you been, all day?" Rosie's aunt bent over her mixing bowl, her quick fingers collecting together the pastry crumbs.

"Freezing out there with all that snow," Rosie replied. "I can think of better ways to spend Good Friday."

"The news has been talking about that American woman and the new King. Mrs Simpson." Nora grimly emphasised her title. "How that'll end, I don't know."

"I went up to the holiday camp." Rosie sat down, playing with her scarlet scarf. "Butlin's? It opens tomorrow.

"You know," she prompted, "the place that's got the funfair. With the zoo and those dodgems you liked?"

Her aunt grunted.

"It looks lovely and you can stay for a whole week," Rosie added.

"Oh?" Nora didn't look up as the rolling pin began its work.

"I did tell you!" Rosie urged, pulling off her overcoat. "Amy Johnson is going to be there."

"Amy . . . ?" The vagueness of Nora's tone made it clear that she was only half-listening.

"Amy Johnson." Rosie breathed her admiration. "The first woman to fly solo from England to Australia! She'll do the grand opening."

"Oh, right." Nora lifted a pastry sheet over the pie dish.

"I saw a notice in the paper," Rosie went on, "saying they're looking for girls."

"Looking for girls!" Nora looked like she would have put her hands on her hips if they weren't dusty. "Cleaning? You know I promised your mother if you came here I'd look after you."

"They want helpers for the guests," Rosie explained.

"Helpers?" The older woman raised a sceptical eyebrow. "Just you make sure what you're getting yourself into."

Rosie helped herself to the teapot, warming her fingers.

"Is the factory not good enough for you any more?" Nora looked up from trimming the pie crust and wiped her hands.

"There's no contest," Rosie informed her pertly. "I'm finished there. It's no distance up to Ingoldmells, and the pay's better, plus food and board is included."

She tallied it up on her fingers, adding, as if in justification, "Ever

Illustration: Pat Gregory

Set in
1936

so many girls were trying out, but I got through to the last ten. I start tomorrow."

The young woman folded herself over the kitchen table, resting her forehead on the warm wood.

Her black hair tumbled around her pink-cheeked face.

"I so want to be an actress, Auntie," she murmured dreamily. "I know that's not what Butlin's is about, but there's a real stage.

"I've seen it in the canteen." She lifted her head to assure her aunt. "There'll be entertainments, dancing and all. I reckon I might be able to persuade them to let me sing."

She hugged herself at the prospect.

"This could be my chance. Mum would be so proud if she was here."

"You think you'll be paid to sing?" Nora looked unconvinced.

Rosie refused to be chastened by the dubious gleam in her eye.

"I know the real work will be looking after the guests," she conceded.

"How are you going to help with that?"

Rosie shrugged.

"Pointing them to the canteen if they're lost, I suppose," she suggested.

"Or reminding them when the 'Bonnie Baby' or 'Knobbly Knees' contests are about to start," she improvised, remembering events that had been mentioned.

The oven door snapped closed and Nora crossed her arms in

> silent disapproval of a perfectly good factory job given up.

Rosie ignored her.

"I'm to be there first thing tomorrow morning," she announced. "Only a hundred guests for the first week apparently, but we still need to give everyone a real Butlin's welcome.

"I'll be shown the chalet where I'm to sleep. Will you walk up with me, Auntie?"

●　●　●　●

Barely after sunrise next morning, niece and aunt clumped through the slush towards the Skegness holiday camp.

"You shan't be dancing much in those boots." Nora laughed, stamping hard to dislodge snow.

"I've brought shoes, too."

Rosie shook her canvas bag, cheerfully impervious to the cold wind whistling in from the North Sea.

"Morning, Mr Cooper," she sang out at the gate.

"Bright and early." He nodded. "I like that."

Alan Cooper was the well-built site manager, whose friendly face Rosie had instinctively trusted.

"Rosie, isn't it?"

"Yes, sir, and this is my aunt Nora," Rosie introduced.

The older woman gave a respectful nod before sliding to one side.

Meanwhile, Alan's attention had already transferred to a shorter, rounder man in a three-piece suit.

Billy Butlin twitched his moustache in dissatisfaction at the uncooperative climate and barked instructions in a strange accent at workmen who scurried to complete a job.

"Just last-minute teething problems, sir." Alan strode over to reassure him. "It'll be sorted. We've plenty of time.

"And look." He beckoned to Rosie who approached warily. "Here's one of your newest staff on the welcoming team. Rosie here is keen as mustard."

Rosie was torn but decided to bob a tiny curtsey, looking the boss straight in the eye.

"Good morning, sir."

Mr Butlin roared with laughter.

"She's a find, Alan," he guffawed, bouncing on the balls of his feet. "No need for 'sir', Rosie, from an enthusiastic girl like you. Call me Guv'nor like everyone else.

"You'll do all right. Just make our guests feel like they're having fun. Friendly faces – that's what you're here for, red Rosie – to brighten up their day."

Unsure whether this was rhetorical, Rosie risked a "thank you", biting back the "sir" that jumped to her lips.

Mr Butlin nodded at his own wise pronouncement and swept off.

"I read what he said in the paper," Nora recalled. "That the Guv'nor was in Barry Island and saw families on their holidays, paying for drab guest-houses and having nothing to do.

"He wanted a place where the whole family enjoys the time together. Bright and colourful. Everything on-site: accommodation, meals, swimming pools, games."

"Clever girl. You made a good impression." Alan nodded

approvingly to Rosie. "Now come with me and let's round up the rest of your little welcoming team."

He looked at his watch.

"I just need to check any last things to do before we get to the station to meet the first arrivals."

• • • •

As she told her aunt later, Rosie took care to soak up as much background as she could from Alan.

"He met Mr Butlin at the races in 1929," she explained. "He's known him ages. He says the Guv'nor was born abroad. That's why he sometimes talks funny.

"He fought in the Great War for Canada, then the Guv'nor worked his passage by ship to England from there. Fancy that!"

"What are the guests like, and the place?" Nora asked impatiently.

"The chalets are ever so nice," her niece enthused. "Six hundred of them. Painted soft blue and pink, each with a little garden."

"Not that you'll see it under the snow," Nora commented wryly.

• • • •

"How did the three-legged racego?" Alan asked Rosie.

It occurred to her that she had somehow become spokeswoman for "her" welcoming team.

"No-one seemed put off by the cold," she reported. "Lads from York won and everyone clapped the sports' day prize-giving.

"Although, afterwards . . ." Rosie faltered. How could she put it to Alan? "There was tea and cake ready, but everyone just drifted away."

She bit her lip, fearing it was somehow her fault.

"Everyone went back to their chalets. In fact, none of the guests has asked me anything. I don't think they know my name from that first day, Alan. Most have forgotten we're even here for them."

Alan sat down hard on a chair, looking deflated.

"I know what you mean," he agreed, and Rosie's heart sank.

Was she about to be sacked after less than a week?

"It was your night off yesterday, but I went into the canteen for their tea."

"Yes?" Rosie thought about her dreams of putting on a show. Dare she suggest it?

Alan was already going on.

"I got up on stage, captive audience an' all, to remind them about the facilities. Like the Guv'nor said, I gave 'em a daily rundown of what's planned."

Rosie pressed her lips together to keep inside her suggestion of a sing-song.

"My jokes went down well as usual," Alan went on, cupping his tea, "but I got talking to a few families afterwards. This woman said they were enjoying themselves all right, but she could never find a face they recognised to answer questions."

"Oh!" Rosie saw the reason for his disappointment. "We're always around but, if you don't know us, I suppose it's easy to mistake us for guests."

"You're right," he mused. "No-one would want to bother another guest."

Rosie saw her moment at last.

"Should we all go on stage, too, ➤

do you think?" she suggested cautiously. "So campers recognise us, like they recognise you?"

"Hmm, yes." Alan drummed his fingers thoughtfully.

"And if we need always to be visible . . ." Rosie started. "To stand out, I mean."

Thinking of Billy Butlin's words when she first met him, she added under her breath, "Bright and colourful".

"Bright and colourful, the Guv'nor said?" she repeated out loud.

Alan slapped his knees.

"You do need to stand out! A uniform, so everyone can see you and know you."

Rosie cast around the room for inspiration.

"Coloured hats maybe?"

Alan's eyes widened as if considering her suggestion.

"Not hats," he said firmly, then broke into a smile. "I'm going to run it past the Guv'nor, but I know he'll love it. Rosie, we're going shopping. I've an idea!"

• • • •

Nora had feigned disinterest when Rosie came home for her day's break, but her niece could see she was desperate for the rest of the tale.

"What did Mr Butlin say? Everyone in town's talking about it," she asked.

Rosie pressed down her grin. She could bet they were. She'd been tasked with bringing another five people to her welcoming team.

"Well," Rosie said, making sure her coat was buttoned to the throat. "Alan went to see the Guv'nor. He drove us to the drapers and we bought some fabric. Pale blue, pink and white."

"Like the chalets," Nora said brightly.

Rosie smiled. Now she knew her aunt had been paying attention.

"Yes, except the Guv'nor apparently didn't like those."

Rosie frowned to remember.

"He wanted a cheerful holiday colour, like you see on the beach, and we must make sure the campers know who we are."

"So what happened?" her aunt prompted.

"Alan and I went to see him together," Rosie explained. "Alan got me to explain my idea about all of the helpers taking part in shows and skits on stage, so they'd get to know us."

Nora clapped in delight.

"Just like you wanted. Well done!"

"Yes, but all the Guv'nor did was stare at my scarf," Rosie said. "Then he clapped his hands."

Nora sat up straighter, curiosity written on her face.

"He said, 'Rosie-red. Like the Mounties!'" her niece recalled. "He had this big grin, like he was remembering something nice."

Finally Rosie unbuttoned her coat, revealing what she wore underneath.

Her aunt smiled with pride.

"We're all to wear red blazers." Rosie gave a slow twirl. "I suggested that my team has a name, so the Guv'nor himself has named us.

"You, Auntie," Rosie continued, unable to contain her excitement a moment longer, "are looking at the new Entertainments Director and leader of the Butlin's Redcoats!" ◾

GREYFRIARS BOBBY

GREYFRIARS BOBBY, a Skye terrier, became a legend for his unwavering loyalty to his owner, John Gray. After John's death in 1858, Bobby refused to leave his master's grave in Edinburgh's Greyfriars Kirkyard, enduring harsh weather conditions for 14 years. His dedication touched the hearts of Edinburgh's citizens, who provided him with shelter and food.

Bobby's story captured the public's imagination, leading to a statue being erected in his honor. However, visitors are now urged to refrain from rubbing his nose, as it causes damage to the statue.

Bobby's grave remains a popular pilgrimage site and his story continues to be told through films and books.

Image: Shutterstock.

A Blessing In Disguise

BY STEFANIA HARTLEY

UNLESS we find some generous donors, we will have to close down," Sister Mary Magdalene, the prioress, admitted.

Silence fell on the common room of the retirement home for nuns.

"But where will we go?"

"Those of us who can move in with family will do that. The others will go to ordinary nursing homes," Sister Mary Magdalene explained.

"But we won't have a chapel or a community to pray with," Sister Teresa pointed out.

"And we will be separated," Sister Joanna added.

"We won't let that happen!" Sister Catherine exclaimed.

Sister Catherine had built three orphanages in Rwanda and two hospitals in Peru, and she wasn't daunted by anything.

"We'll do God's will, Sister, as we have always done," Sister Mary Magdalene replied.

"But being separated might not be God's will," Sister Joanna said quietly.

"You're right. For the rest of this week, we're going to pray

that we may discover God's will for us and receive the means to do it."

For the following few days, puzzles, knitting and crosswords were abandoned, and even some of the everyday chores slipped a little, but the chapel was never empty.

The overwhelming consensus was that God's will was that they should stay.

"Then we must find some donors," Sister Mary Magdalene declared.

"How about we raise some money ourselves? I could give herbal medicine classes," Sister Catherine suggested.

"I could knit and sell baby hats and booties," Sister Pascal added, taking her knitting needles out of her bag.

"And I could bake shortbread with my grandmother's recipe," Sister Teresa offered.

Sister Joanna looked at her gnarled hands and sighed.

"I can't think of anything I can do."

"You could offer prayers," Sister Catherine said.

"No. Prayers we will always do for free," Sister Mary Magdalene

Illustration by Jim Dewar.

said categorically.

"Sister Joanna could do story sessions for children," Sister Teresa suggested.

"My eyes aren't up to reading," Sister Joanna replied.

"Then you could offer listening," Sister Agatha suggested quietly.

"Who's going to want that?" Sister Joanna asked.

Sister Mary Magdalene smiled.

"I imagine plenty of people would want that. We can only try."

• • • •

As soon as the notice went up on the village noticeboard,

people turned up at the nuns' door.

A few children were signed up for Storytime with the Prioress, a few baskets of biscuits were purchased, and a couple of knitted items were sold.

But the bookings list for Sister Joanna's listening appointments filled more than two A4 pages of her notebook.

"There must be a misunderstanding," she reasoned. "Surely all these people think that I'll solve their problems, but I can't.

"I can't even give advice. I'm not a trained counsellor," Sister Joanna fretted.

➤

"Don't worry. We've made it very clear. They don't expect anything other than being listened to," Sister Mary Magdalene assured her. "Do you think you can do that?"

"I think so."

Sister Joanna must have done her job very well because, after two days, her bookings filled four pages.

Rich and poor, old and young, individuals and couples – all kinds of people had signed up.

Some were already booking their second and third appointments, while others had come from neighbouring villages and towns because of word of mouth, and some were just curious.

Sister Catherine had to be deployed on phone duty to take the vast number of appointment requests.

Meanwhile, the other nuns were knitting, baking and assembling pot-pourris, but the sales were low.

Sister Joanna, meanwhile, was so busy that she struggled to protect her prayer time and rest.

"Each one of us should stop doing what they're doing and help Sister Joanna," Sister Teresa suggested.

Everyone agreed, and even Sister Pascal offered herself for listening duties.

"So long as my hearing aid's battery lasts," she said with a chuckle.

The listening service was so in demand that, despite the appointments being very reasonably priced, the nuns were collecting enough income to stave off closure.

Even Sister Mary Magdalene left her prioress duties and was on the listening roster several times a week.

Sister Mary Magdalene was listening to a client venting about her lacklustre marriage.

"So, Sister, what should I do?" the woman asked.

Until then, nobody had asked her for advice.

They had been very clear about it when they had advertised their services.

"I'm sorry. We don't give advice."

"But the article on the newspaper said that you do," the woman pointed out.

"Which article?"

This was how she learned that a newspaper had published an article about their listening service.

As soon as she finished that session, Sister Mary Magdalene rushed to buy a copy.

But she soon wished she never had.

Home-wrecking Nuns, read the title of the article.

Sister Mary Magdalene had to sit down and drink a glass of water before she could read any more.

A disgruntled husband complained that his wife had left him after a session with Sister Joanna, during which, so the wife told him, her eyes had been opened and she had made up her mind to end their relationship.

"I remember that young woman," Sister Joanna told her. "I didn't give her any advice at all. I just listened, like always.

"At one point, she exclaimed, 'I

know what I've got to do!'.

"Then she got up and left," Sister Joanna finished.

The sisters decided that the newspaper must hear their side of the story.

Sister Mary Magdalene penned a simple press release, picked up the phone and rang the newspaper office.

"We would love to publish your side of the story!" the editor answered enthusiastically.

"Good. Have you got pen and paper?" Sister Mary Magdalene asked, ready to dictate her press release.

"Of course, and we'll also have voice recorders and photographers."

Oh, no, this wasn't what she had in mind.

"How about a phone interview?" she suggested instead.

"Readers want to see how nuns live, what they do all day and why," the editor replied. "We'll do a long feature about you, if that's OK."

The thought of journalists snooping inside their home and prying into their lives made Sister Mary Magdalene shudder, but if there was no other way to correct the misinformation about their services, they would have to do it.

"Only if we get to read and approve the article before publication."

"That's fine."

• • • •

Every corner of their home had been scrubbed to sparkling, every habit and veil had been ironed and every prayer had been said by the time the newspaper crew arrived.

The sisters were shy at first, but then soon relaxed a bit, and the photographer took photos of them doing the usual chores while the journalist interviewed them.

Then the wait began.

For a whole day, the sisters waited breathlessly to receive the draft of the article.

When it finally arrived, they gathered in the common room and opened the brown envelope.

Sister Mary Magdalene read it aloud.

"They've called morning lauds an 'ancient practice'," Sister Catherine objected.

"Did I hear correctly that they called my knitting 'kitsch'?" Sister Pascal asked.

"I don't think the décor of our home is antiquated," Sister Teresa complained.

"Let us concentrate on the things that matter and exercise humility on the rest," Sister Mary Magdalene suggested.

Everyone nodded.

Sister Mary Magdalene read the article aloud one more time, and they all agreed that it was acceptable for publication.

As soon as their copy of the newspaper arrived, Sister Mary Magdalene called everyone for a meeting.

This was the moment of truth: if the editor had published something different and betrayed them, they'd find out now.

The article was on the second page of the newspaper, accompanied by several large photographs of the sisters occupied in their daily activities.

Sister Teresa was ironing, Sister Pascal was doing her daily round of the cloister, and the whole community were singing morning lauds in the chapel.

The text of the article was exactly what they had approved, but there was a little surprise, too.

Up on the top right corner, a box contained quotes from people who had used their listening services.

"I don't want to know what it says," Sister Joanna cried, covering her ears.

"Neither do I." Sister Pascal agreed, turning down her hearing aid.

Sister Mary Magdalene pushed her glasses up her nose.

"We must."

The people interviewed reported that they left the listening sessions feeling calmer and more at peace with themselves and the world.

"I needed to talk to someone who isn't emotionally involved, unlike my family or my friends," a teenage girl confided.

"Putting feelings into words made me understand myself better," a young man said.

"The nuns don't tell you how to solve your problems, but just talking things out gives you clarity on your situation," a mother of four said.

"I was very lonely until I found the nuns to talk to," a divorced father said.

"I didn't realise that we were doing so much good," Sister Teresa admitted.

"To think it all started because Sister Joanna thought she couldn't do anything useful!"

Sister Catherine exclaimed.

"Actually, it all started because we were about to close down," Sister Mary Magdalene reminded everyone. "Trials and trouble often bring better things."

• • • •

It was again Sister Mary Magdalene's turn to sit for the listening appointments.

A young woman walked into the parlour and greeted her with a bright smile.

Sister Mary Magdalene was surprised: clients usually looked happy after their appointments, not before.

"I'm not sure a listening appointment is the right thing for what I need to talk about, but I booked it anyway because I needed to see you.

"I've read the article on the newspaper and I'm fascinated by all the good you and the sisters have done," the girl said with sparkly eyes.

Sister Mary Magdalene smiled.

"Yes, we've all spent our lives helping others in every continent of the world.

"Some of us have worked in orphanages, schools –"

"I mean, all the good you've done in the last month," the girl interrupted her. "How you make people feel better just by listening to them and being there for them."

"Oh."

"And I feel called to do the same," she continued. "Sister Mary Magdalene, please, can I join you?"

Sister Mary Magdalene smiled.

The Lord works in mysterious ways, she thought. ❖

Dew On A Spider's Web

Bright early morning sun reveals
A garden kissed with dew,
Where sparkling droplets light the lawn
And fall from flowers, too.

But higher than them all,
Suspended from two budding stems,
The dew has kissed a spider's web
With dazzling silver gems.

I fetch my camera and step out,
Through damp grass, to the place
Where I can photograph this piece
Of perfect, jewelled lace.

Susannah White

Illustration by Shutterstock

Words On Paper

BY VIVIEN BROWN

NOBODY writes letters these days," Gerry said ruefully as he shook his head, carefully re-tied the string that held the bundle together and slipped it back into a drawer.

He still missed Barbara, but reading her words again, her small, neat writing laid out on her usual pale pink paper, and seeing the little kisses she used to draw on the back of the envelopes always cheered him up.

He sometimes imagined he could still smell her perfume whenever he unwrapped the treasured letters, but he was probably just being fanciful.

"It's the cost of the stamps, I suppose."

His daughter Lizzie handed him a cup of tea and settled beside him on the sofa, balancing a plate of biscuits on her lap.

"And then there's having to go out to the postbox in all weathers!" she added. "It can take days, sometimes, for a letter to arrive, even when you pay the extra for first-class post.

"People can't be bothered with all that any more," she went on. "Not when e-mails and texts are so much easier and quicker."

"Oh, I know that, love," Gerry admitted. "You can't stand in the way of progress, and my silver surfer lessons at the library have been a godsend, but e-mails just aren't the same as putting pen to paper, are they?

"I mean, who looks back over old e-mails and re-reads them? That's if you can find the ones you want amongst all the junk mail we all get sent these days.

"I had one last week, supposedly from the telephone company, riddled with spelling mistakes," he added. "I might be getting on a bit, but I know a scam when I see one."

"I'd like to see any scammer try to get one past you, Dad!" Lizzie laughed.

"Dating for the over-seventies – that's the latest messages I keep getting." Gerry took a digestive and dipped it into his cup of tea. "How do they know who to target? That's what I'd like to know."

"Just delete them, Dad, or mark them as spam." She put her hand on his knee. "Don't let it upset you."

"Oh, I'm not upset by it, but there's no way I'm looking for love again at my time of life.

Illustration: Kirk Houston.

"Besides, I've got you and the girls. That's all the love I need."

"Talking of which," Lizzie replied, "Laura and Jenny want to know what we can get you for Father's Day this year."

Gerry looked thoughtful.

"There's nothing I need, love," he said finally. "And I certainly don't expect anything.

"A pair of socks will be fine. Or some of those toffees I like – but from you, not the girls.

"Tell them to save their money. It's Father's Day and the clue's in the name! I'm their grandfather, not their dad."

"Since when has that mattered?" Lizzie pointed out.

"They see so little of Jim since he shot off to Canada with wife number two, and Father's Day isn't just for biological fathers these days.

"So many kids have stepdads, adopted dads, uncles or godfathers who they want to say thank you to," she reminded him. "Have a think about it anyway. It's still a week away."

Gerry sipped his tea and let his mind drift back to his courting days.

Oh, how he had loved his Barbara!

By some miracle, she had felt the same way.

He would never have become a

father or a grandfather if it hadn't been for her.

It was not as if Barbara's widowed mum had had a phone in the house back then, let alone one of these modern mobiles.

There were no calls or texts, and certainly no e-mails when they were love-struck teenagers, hardly older than the twins were now.

And a paper round didn't bring in enough money to catch the bus over to see her more than once a week.

He'd wanted to save up enough for their monthly date, with two back-row seats at the pictures, a bag of sweets and an ice-cream to share in the interval.

It was walks in the park or an evening on her mum's sofa watching TV on the weekends in between.

Even when he'd got his first proper job at the garage, he hadn't earned enough for it to make a lot of difference – not in the first year or so anyway.

No, letters had been important back then.

A lifeline, he supposed you could call them, keeping them connected when they were apart.

And they weren't sent off in haste, packed with errors, the way e-mails seemed to be.

You took your time, using your best pen and your best handwriting and carefully choosing just the right words.

If you made a mistake, you would just screw the whole thing up and start again.

His wastepaper bin had regularly been piled high with discarded letters he had never finished, let alone sent.

Barbara would write every Sunday, straight after their Saturday meeting, and post the letter first thing on Monday morning.

Sometimes it would even arrive the same afternoon.

Oh, how he longed for the return of two deliveries a day!

Her letter only had to travel 12 miles, from her home village to his parents' council house in town, but it might as well have been 100 when it came to getting to see each other.

It was too far to walk and his parents could never afford to buy him a bike.

Gerry knew he was not as good a writer as she was.

He had struggled at school, being more of a practical fix-it kind of a fellow than a bookish one, yet still he made sure to write back every time, posting his letter on a Wednesday so she would receive it before their next Saturday date.

He did wonder sometimes if they would find enough to write about.

It wasn't as if either of them led particularly exciting lives, yet seeing that letter land on the door mat every week was always exciting in itself.

"Is there anything else I can do before I head off?" Lizzie's voice cut into his daydreams. "Would you like me to run the vacuum round or pop some washing into the machine?"

Gerry opened his eyes. He hadn't realised he had closed them.

Maybe he had nodded off for a moment there.

"No, I'm fine, and I'm more than capable of washing my own

smalls! No, you get off. The twins will be back from swimming soon, won't they? And then revising again, no doubt.

"Go and get them fed," he added. "I'll see you next Sunday as usual."

"OK, Dad," Lizzie replied with a grin. "I'll call you in the week. See if you've had any thoughts about your present."

"I told you –" he began.

"I know you did," she cut in, "but I don't always take no for an answer. I wonder who I got that from?"

She laughed and picked up her cardigan from the armchair, then bent to kiss him on the cheek before letting herself out of the house.

• • • •

"But we can't buy him socks!"

Laura stood with her hands on her hips, looking remarkably like her grandmother Barbara when she had been in one of her indignant moods.

"We got him socks on his birthday," she went on, "and there's only so many a person can possibly need,"

"You're right," Jenny chipped in, pulling a brush through her still-damp hair. "It has to be something more thoughtful, something he'll really like."

"Such as?" Laura asked.

"I have no idea. But we can make him a card while we think about it. Have we still got any glitter left over from Christmas?"

Laura shrugged.

"I'm not sure Grandad's a glitter kind of person."

"Hearts, then?"

"It's not Valentine's Day," Laura said, smirking. "Save the hearts for Sean Fuller."

"What do you mean?" Jenny spluttered, her face rapidly turning a rather bright shade of pink.

"Oh, come on. Everyone knows you fancy him, and you've been texting each other," Laura teased her sister. "You'll be slipping him love notes under the table in the exams next!"

"What?" Jenny gasped. "Passing pieces of paper around in an exam would get me chucked out and accused of cheating.

"And I don't fancy him anyway. We just text about school stuff. He's my revision partner for maths . . ."

"If you say so." Laura eyed her mischievously.

"Enough of all that," Lizzie said, coming into the room with their dinner. "But I think you might just have hit on the perfect gift for Grandad."

"We have?" the girls asked in unison.

She nodded.

"I found him reading your gran's old letters again today," their mother explained. "It got me thinking.

"He misses it, receiving letters and writing them. I know it seems old-fashioned nowadays, but he really treasures those old letters. They bring back memories – good ones.

"Maybe you could write to him? He's seen so little of you lately while the GCSEs have been on, and he'd love to hear all your news."

"But we e-mail him," Jenny pointed out. "Since he did that course he knows how to open attachments now and save the photos we send him."

"I know." Lizzie nodded. "But he's not keen on e-mails or digital photos. Not when it comes to family stuff. It's OK to get his gas bill that way, but he'd much prefer something on real paper in your own writing.

"Maybe we could add a printed photo or two?" Lizzie added. "He could pin them on the board in the kitchen or put one in a frame."

Whilst their mother spoke, the girls ate their dinner in silence.

"But what would we say?" Laura asked, picking up the conversation again as she took the dirty plates out to the kitchen. "I've never written an actual letter before."

"Whatever you think he'd like to hear," Lizzie replied. "How the exams are going, what you did in swimming club, what you've seen on TV. It doesn't have to be wildly exciting stuff, just your everyday lives.

"I think he'd really like that, and all it will cost is the price of a stamp."

• • • •

"Happy Father's Day, Grandad!" the girls chorused as they burst into their grandad's the following Sunday afternoon.

"'Oh, it's lovely to see you both!" Gerry exclaimed. "And thank you so much for the letter."

He nodded in the direction of the sideboard where the letter, tucked back inside its flowery envelope, sat in pride of place.

"I'm glad the exams are going so well," he added. "Last couple this week, eh?"

Lizzie smiled to herself.

Her idea had been a success, then.

She drew the wrapped present out from behind her back and handed it to her dad.

"For you."

"Well, it's the wrong shape for socks!" Gerry grinned as he pulled at the wrapping paper. "Oh, it's a writing set."

"Yes, posh paper and envelopes, a new pen and a sheet of stamps, too," Lizzie told him. "If your granddaughters are going to be writing you letters, I thought you might like to write back every now and then."

Gerry looked up at Laura and Jenny expectantly.

"Really? Can I?" he asked. "Would you like that?'

The girls both nodded.

It had actually been fun deciding what to tell him and what to keep quiet about (Sean Fuller, for one).

Even walking down to the postbox had provided a short break from their revision and a breath of fresh air.

"And what's this, then?" Gerry asked, pulling something small and coiled up from what was left of his parcel.

"String, Dad," Lizzie replied. "If you're going to be receiving letters again . . ."

She looked over to the drawer where she knew he kept all the letters he'd ever received from Mum.

". . . then I have a feeling that you will be wanting to keep them.

"And we both know there's nothing like a good piece of strong string to bundle them all together."

BARRY ISLAND, VALE OF GLAMORGAN

THE seaside town of Barry, famous for its association with the sitcom "Gavin & Stacey," has a rich history beyond its television fame. In the 1960s, it was a popular seaside destination with a bustling funfair and the iconic Butlin's holiday camp.

The town's industrial past is equally fascinating, having once been the world's largest coal port. The remnants of this era can be seen in the historic docklands and the grand architecture of the town centre.

Beyond Barry, the surrounding area offers a wealth of attractions. Dyffryn Gardens, a stunning botanical garden, showcases a diverse range of plant life. The historic village of Llancarfan boasts a medieval church with hidden medieval murals. And the coastal village of Rhoose is home to Cardiff Airport and the historic site where Guglielmo Marconi conducted groundbreaking radio experiments.

Whether you're a fan of the show or simply seeking a nostalgic seaside escape, Barry and its surrounding areas offer a unique blend of history, culture and coastal beauty.

The Sands Of North Berwick

BY CHRISTOPHER GOULDING

TWO hundred and fifty pounds is a tidy sum of money, Mrs Mullen. You're wise to take it in the form of a cheque."

Fiona Mullen nodded in polite acknowledgement of this compliment at the man sitting behind the desk in the grand wood-panelled room high above Waverley Station.

Sitting awkwardly in her chair, she glanced around at the framed maps, engineering diagrams and oil paintings of grand steam locomotives that adorned the walls.

Behind the desk loomed a large clock, whose big black hands pointed at Roman numerals that defied contradiction.

"In these circumstances there's always a temptation for the bereaved families of staff paid weekly in cash to take it in the form of gold sovereigns," he added with an air of distaste.

He looked at her over the top of his gold-rimmed spectacles.

Fiona winced as the piercing steam whistle of a departing train came from the window that overlooked the platforms below.

It was a stark reminder that "these circumstances" were the recent death of her husband, Sandy, a signalman with the railway company, and the compensation she was to be paid, further to the verdict of the fiscal's inquest.

The man's face softened as he took a steel pocket watch and chain from his desk drawer and reverently handed it to her.

"Your late husband's watch. Company property, of course, but we thought you might like it as a keepsake . . ."

Fiona took the fine polished steel watch, opened the cover and saw the company logo on the face and her late husband's name engraved inside the hinged cover.

She noted that it told exactly the same time as the clock on the wall.

Someone had kept it wound up, she thought, as it ticked away the minutes by which the great railway network outside operated.

At the inquest they'd said it was an error of only 30 seconds in the timing of a points-change that had led to Sandy being in the wrong place at the wrong time.

Indeed, a mail train had emerged from the tunnel as he was crossing the track from the signal box at the end of his shift that terrible morning.

Illustration: Sailesh Thakrar.

Set in 1890

The man behind the desk shifted uncomfortably in his chair, glancing unsurely at Fiona.

"Speaking of company property," he continued, "I'm afraid your tenancy of the company housing must be terminated."

Fiona had known this was coming.

Their three poky little rooms in the company tenement over in Haymarket would be needed for another railway family.

As a mere widow with no working man, she and her child would need to be dispensed with.

Watching the expression on her face, the man seemed moved to sympathy.

"No rush, of course," he told her. "We can give you a month to make alternative arrangements."

He reached across his desk to hand her the cheque.

"This should make things a little easier. And then there's the pension, of course."

The pension.

Fiona knew that with Sandy having been a young man with only eight years' service, that the pension wouldn't be much.

Placing the cheque in her handbag, Fiona rose from her chair.

She needed to get out of this

stifling room.

The man rose, too, and held out his hand.

"You'll be able to open an account at any bank with that cheque."

Fiona nodded politely and turned to leave as the man dashed around his desk to open the office door for her.

A bank! That would be a change from Sandy placing his wages in cash on the kitchen table every Friday evening, she thought as she strode out of the room.

In the outer office, her six-year-old daughter Flora sat waiting under the watchful eye of a typist.

"Mummy, can we go there one day?" the little girl asked with a smile, pointing at a railway poster on the wall.

It was a gaily coloured scene showing happy holidaymakers on a beach, with people playing golf in the background.

North Berwick, it said in large letters at the bottom, next to the railway company's logo.

Why not, Fiona thought. She and her daughter had been through a lot in recent weeks.

It was sunny outside and she knew she still had a few pounds in her purse left over from the hardship payment Sandy's union had given her.

"Come on, then, Flora. Let's go," she said. "There's no time like the present."

•　•　•　•

As the train rattled its way along the line, Fiona watched her daughter press her nose against the carriage window, her eyes fixed on the moving scenery outside as they left Edinburgh behind.

Fiona's eyes also strayed to look outward as huddled streets turned into green fields and an early glimpse of the sea as they passed tantalisingly close to the coast at Musselburgh.

As the train made its way around a long curve, she saw the track glinting in the sun as it stretched into the distance before them.

No points or junctions on this line, she mused, thinking of what would have been Sandy's professional point of view: straight to North Berwick and beyond.

What would the future bring?

She had one month's grace before she and Flora had to leave their home . . .

Was that enough time to start a new life?

With neither her nor Sandy's parents still around, Fiona knew that she and her daughter were on their own.

Rummaging in her handbag, she took out Sandy's watch and looked at it.

Glancing back at her bag, she noticed the cheque inside.

What on earth was she to do with such an enormous king's ransom of a sum?

Soon the train pulled into North Berwick station and they made their way down into the town.

It was a fine day, and the two visitors were greeted by the fresh scent of the sea that breezed up from the beach.

What a change from their home in Auld Reekie, Fiona thought.

Walking down towards the

small high street, Fiona noticed the neat cottages they were passing, some with a small patch of garden before them.

They looked like cosy wee homes, she thought.

The sound of children's voices sang across the rooftops from a school hidden somewhere behind them.

Where the road met with the high street, there was a crossroads with a small, cobbled square on the far side, and beyond that Fiona could see the beach.

On the corner overlooking the square was a small newsagent's shop.

Fiona knew there would be a report of the inquest in the local paper, which she wanted to read, as most of the proceedings had been a sad blur for her whilst she'd been there.

Crossing the road to the shop, she noticed the shop was also a confectioner and general dealer, with a selection of sweets, bric-a-brac and novelties for tourists in the window.

On the doorframe hung a selection of coloured small metal buckets and spades for children.

Seeing the first gleam she'd noted in Flora's eyes for weeks, Fiona unhooked a bucket and spade as they walked in.

At the counter stood a sad-looking elderly lady, who nonetheless gave a warm smile as they entered.

Behind her an open doorway revealed a cosy sitting-room with an armchair by a fireplace, above which a carriage clock ticked on the mantelpiece.

On the wall above that, Fiona saw a framed portrait photograph of an elderly man, draped with black mourning ribbons.

A recent widow, like me, Fiona thought – though one who'd enjoyed more of married life than her.

She asked for a copy of the "East Lothian Chronicle" and then, looking down at Flora, saw her daughter's eyes fixed on the rows of loose sweets displayed on the counter.

"I'll spend the change on a selection of those sweets, please," Fiona said, handing over two shillings.

●　●　●　●

A quarter of an hour later, Fiona was walking along the beach, her daughter skipping ahead before her.

As the waves receded from the tide-dampened sand, she looked out at Bass Rock, standing like a fortress dominating the Firth of Forth.

Turning her head inland, she saw its landlocked twin Berwick Law, looming behind the town.

She remembered from lessons at school that these – like Arthur's Seat and Castle Rock back in Edinburgh – were the remains of pre-historic volcanoes.

Just up ahead on the beach there were small, rocky outcrops of dark-grey pumice stone: ancient lava, frozen in time.

One rock, worn smooth by the sea, looked comfortable enough to sit on.

Settling down, as Flora chased low-flying seagulls, Fiona glanced at the newspaper she'd bought, finding the report of the inquest on page five.

It was quite brief, the details of

the tragedy and the verdict succinctly reduced to half a dozen paragraphs.

Wincing at the memories it brought back, Fiona turned the page and her eye was caught by a column headlined with the familiar quotation, *An Englishman's home is his castle.*

The first paragraph revealed it to be a story about a tenant farmer near Dalkeith who came from south of the border in dispute with his landlord, who wanted him out.

Fiona had heard the quotation before and sympathised with the farmer who had used it in court.

Thinking of her own circumstances, and the month she had before she lost the company flat in Haymarket, she furrowed her brow.

Why shouldn't a Scots woman's home be her castle, she wondered.

Fiona looked up from the page to the scene around her.

How many millions of years had it taken the relentless action of the sea to carve out this landscape?

Her own future life, even beyond that month, would be measured in mere decades and seemed so short and insignificant in comparison.

Gazing down, she saw a patch of dry sand by her feet.

Taking up a handful, she let it seep out between her fingers and be carried off by the wind.

"How long would it take all of the sand on this beach to pass through an hourglass?" she whispered to herself.

"Mummy, look at the seagulls!"

Startled from her reverie, Fiona looked up to see her daughter chasing a pair of birds that had been waddling along the sand.

"Ach, Flora, leave the poor things alone."

Smiling at her daughter as she scampered after the birds, Fiona glanced back at the newspaper and leafed through a few pages.

The back pages were filled with columns of advertisements.

First came the property pages.

There were long lists of small ads announcing local cottages for rent, which seemed very cheap compared to Edinburgh.

But the cheque in her handbag made her think she might leave the precarious world of tenancy behind and perhaps buy somewhere for long-term security for Flora's sake, as well as her own?

Her eyes were drawn to bigger, boxed notices proclaiming large houses for sale, some even with photographs.

One substantial, detached seafront villa in nearby Gullane was going for £500.

Fiona balked at the price. It was way beyond her means and her £250 cheque.

"A Scots woman's home"? And not so much a castle as a palace!

Fiona knew that wherever she lived, she'd need a job to pay her bills.

That meant staying in Edinburgh, where there would be any amount of opportunities to be had.

Beautiful as North Berwick was, there surely couldn't be any prospects for her here?

Fiona's eyes strayed to the bottom of the page, where a column was headed *Businesses For Sale.*

First on the list was a local newsagent and confectionery shop.

Busy corner site, it said, adding, *Steady year-round local trade, with good tourist novelty sales in summer.*

Looking at the shop's address, Fiona realised that it was the very shop where she'd bought the newspaper.

Further details listed the living-room behind the counter that she'd noticed earlier, along with two bedrooms above.

Fiona looked up from the page and saw her daughter giggling as she ran across the sand, the bucket and spade in her hands.

She breathed in a deep lungful of the fresh seaside air and thought how much better a place this would be to raise a daughter than the smoky back lanes of Haymarket and the stairwells of some Edinburgh tenement.

She looked back at the advertisement.

Freehold £200 (including stock) – priced for quick sale due to proprietor's retirement.

A thrill of excitement ran up Fiona's spine.

She looked up at her daughter, who was now scooping up spadefuls of sand and joyfully throwing them above her into the wind.

Fiona's eyes strayed to the retreating sea beyond, to Bass Rock and to the beach that stretched into the distance on either side of them.

She thought of the rest of her life, lying unseen before her towards a distant future.

She thought of the railway line, shining in the sun, that had brought them here.

She thought of the here and now and the junction at which she found herself.

She thought of the decision she was making that would signal a change of route, of points being changed to send her life down a different line.

She took Sandy's watch out from her handbag and noted the time as the steel of the open lid bearing her late husband's name glinted in the sunlight.

They'd need to return to Edinburgh in an hour or so – she still had a few matters to settle – but after that there would be a one-way ticket back to North Berwick sure enough.

Yet they still had time for a little while on the beach . . .

Her mind made up, Fiona glanced over her shoulder and set her sights firmly on the corner shop, smiling with a hope she hadn't felt for some time.

Then, turning back to the beach, she called for her daughter.

Flora ran cheerfully to her mother, bucket and spade in hand.

"What are we going to do?" the little girl asked.

Fiona smiled at the young face looking up at her.

"Here, give me a go with that spade," she said.

Handing it to her mother, Flora giggled as her mother started to dig up a spadeful of damp sand.

"What are you doing, Mum?"

"Hold out that bucket, Flora," the proud Scots woman answered. "We're going to build ourselves a castle."

Be Still

When sorrow overwhelms you and you have no strength to smile,
When each day is hard to live through and it barely seems worthwhile,
When your voice is close to breaking from the tears you cannot cry,
Just be still,
Be still
And know you are with God.

When the world spins on regardless of your troubles and your pain,
When you wonder if you'll ever laugh or dance with joy again,
When it feels as though your words of prayer are offered up in vain,
Just be still,
Be still
And know you are with God.

When the sun comes slowly rising with the promise of the dawn,
When your sorrows ease and nightmares fade into the golden morn,
When you look upon the world and know your faith has been reborn,
Just be still,
Be still
And know you are with God.

Annaliza Davis

Illustration: Shutterstock.

HAMISH MCHAMISH

HAMISH MCHAMISH, a cat with a heart of gold, became a beloved icon of St Andrews. Though technically owned, Hamish preferred a free-spirited life, roaming the town's streets and making friends wherever he went. His friendly nature and distinctive ginger coat made him instantly recognisable, and he was often seen napping in sunny spots or seeking affection from passers-by.

To honor his legacy, a bronze statue was erected by his fans. This tribute was made possible by a fund-raising campaign started by the local newspaper.

Hamish McHamish, the beloved stray, continues to be cherished by the people of St Andrews, his spirit living on in the hearts of those who knew him.

Image: Alamy.

A Storybook Romance

BY ALISON CARTER

A COPY of "City Success" magazine lay on the coffee table in Rosemary's office. It was the table around which she sat with stars and producers and talked money and fame.

On the front of the magazine was a man she didn't recognise; someone in steel or oil, the headline suggested.

His face filled the glossy rectangle, the image overflowing its edges.

In three months, "City Success" would announce its "Man Of The Year" and its "Woman Of The Year".

The latter had only been awarded for the past two years, and Rosemary had learned that she might be in the running this time.

"Obviously I can't promise, Rosie," Ed Roberts had warned her on the phone from "City Success". "I don't even make the decision. I just advise the Editor from my humble desk.

"But you're looking good for it," he'd added. "What I'd say is, keep up the good work. Make 'The Daughter Of The Highlands'

a huge hit."

Rosemary Pagett was a casting agent.

But she was more than that. She put actors, writers and directors on the map.

At only thirty-eight years old, she was at the very top of her game.

The entertainment industry of the early Sixties was male dominated, but Rosemary could hold her own with the boys.

Now, at the start of 1964, she was branching out.

She had managed to secure the rights to the novel du jour, the book that was piled high in every bookshop's window.

It was a picturesque, passionate, tear-jerking romance that was going to be made into a fabulous film – a film that Rosemary was going to cast better than any blockbuster had ever been cast before.

Ed's words were in her head as she opened her copy of "Spotlight", the actor's directory.

Normally, this weighty tome stayed on her office shelf, because Rosemary always knew who she wanted, and the people that she wanted always answered

Illustration: André Leonard.

the phone.

But this time she was unsure.

To make a mark with "The Daughter Of The Highlands", she had to find someone fresh.

There were a dozen actors who looked right and were the correct age for the forty-something hero.

However, all of them came with baggage, precisely because they were no longer young – a recent divorce, a recent flop, an annoying habit of making directors walk off set . . .

Rosemary's assistant knocked on her open door.

"I'm putting the kettle on," she said. "Want anything?"

"No, thanks. Kitty, have you read 'The Daughter Of The Highlands'?"

"Yes. It's good in its genre," Kitty replied. "I'm surprised they didn't put a picture of the author on the dust jacket."

"Oh?"

"My sister's boyfriend's cousin's friend knows the chap and apparently he's a dish."

Rosemary shook her head.

"This person can't possibly know Colin McDaniel, Kitty. He uses a pseudonym and hasn't revealed his identity.

"It took me weeks just to get a comment about film rights via his literary agent. He's notoriously secretive."

"All I know is what Jane's boyfriend's cousin's friend told me." Kitty shrugged, then left the room.

As she began her day's work, Rosemary could not get certain images out of her head.

If McDaniel was a dish, and if he could be found, there might be a coup in it for her – or more than one.

Tracking down the hottest property in publishing – that would be something!

She might be able to reveal that McDaniel was a romantic hero himself, with the good looks of the laird in his bankable novel.

Rosemary got out her copy of "The Daughter Of The Highlands" and sat back.

She pushed away her "Spotlight" directory to make room, then another thought came to her.

What if he could be prevailed upon to act in the movie?

He was quite likely to be a competent actor – writers often were, in Rosemary's experience.

She had cast writers before with great success.

His novel was packed with strong characters and she could picture him at his desk, acting each scene as he wrote it.

And obviously he knew the lines like the back of his hand.

This could be a publicity stunt of spectacular proportions!

That day, Kitty asked if she could go early to visit a dressmaker.

She was getting married in April and would probably end up leaving to have a baby, which was always annoying.

Rosemary had been married once and that had been a disaster.

Romantic novels were all very well and lucrative, but she had found that real-life relationships were fraught with danger and disappointment.

She knew where her own affections lay – in an admirable career and a healthy bank balance.

● ● ● ●

Rosemary set about finding Colin McDaniel.

She quizzed Kitty about how the gossip had reached her and set to work.

Making contacts was one of Rosemary's skills.

Some phone calls and two letters gave her the vital first link in the chain – the "friend", who turned out to be a dull woman of about thirty who lived south of Oxford in a semi.

The woman, Mrs Pierce, was thrilled to be told that she was assisting in the casting of a film.

She explained that she often walked her dogs in nearby fields, and that one winter morning she had been behind a bush.

"I've got this springer spaniel, Miss Pagett, who's a terror," Mrs Pierce told her. "She will run off!

"Anyway, I heard a man's voice. He couldn't see me. He seemed to be reading a story to himself, or that's what I thought."

She pressed her hands on her knees and leaned forward.

"You'll never guess! I recognised the characters!

"He was acting young Ailsa Beatie from 'The Daughter Of The Highlands'!"

Mrs Pierce reported how she

then leapt out from behind the bush.

"I must have given the gentleman a fright," she laughed. "I asked him, just like that, and he confessed to being Colin McDaniel. But I knew that what he'd been reciting was not 'The Daughter Of The Highlands'!

"I know every word of that book, Miss Pagett. Eventually he admitted that it was the sequel!" Mrs Pierce added. "He said I wasn't to tell a soul, which of course is quite right.

"We don't want the world and his wife knowing the next bit of the story before it comes out, do we?"

"But you did tell," Rosemary pointed out.

Mrs Pierce's face turned pink.

"Only one friend, and she's awfully discreet."

Rosemary nodded. People were always discreet.

"Did you learn anything else about Mr McDaniel?"

"Not a thing."

Rosemary was downhearted. Unless she hung about in the fields for days, she couldn't find the man.

Two minutes later she was standing by the front door.

"FIt was a funny thing, though," Mrs Pierce began, "seeing him again only yesterday."

"Again?" Rosemary repeated.

"He was just going into Magdalen College. I was out buying marmalade, and there he was."

If Colin McDaniel lived in the Oxford college then it would be easy to find him.

The men who came and went through college porter's lodges usually lived there.

Rosemary drove into the city straightaway.

She dug a glove out of her bag and told the porter that she'd seen a man drop it.

"Just before he came in here," she said.

"Can you describe him?" the porter asked.

"Definitely too old to be an undergraduate." Rosemary frowned. "Golly . . . very nice looking, I suppose I'd say."

A girl standing at the mail pigeon holes turned round.

"That's got to be Professor Randall, Eng Literature. There's only one handsome man here."

A professor! This was getting better and better.

The porter went off to fetch Professor Randall so that Rosemary could hand back the glove.

"We don't let ladies wander about the college on their own," he said.

"Naturally." Rosemary nodded.

• • • •

Professor Randall came striding across the quad five minutes later, with the porter hurrying along behind.

He looked startlingly like Peter O'Toole, but wearing ill-fitting tweedy trousers and with his hair unkempt.

Rosemary had time to observe that the 1960s were passing this man by, and apparently so had the 1950s, but there was currency in his look.

The laird in "The Daughter Of The Highlands" was one of those sexy heroes who looks as though he doesn't care about anything ❯

or anybody, before falling for the girl.

The professor was horrified at what Rosemary had to say.

"I don't know where you got this information from," he said indignantly.

"But it's true? You are Colin McDaniel?"

"I have a tutorial to deliver," he said.

Rosemary was not to be fobbed off so easily.

She tailed him into the cloisters, talking all the way.

"No, I don't think I'd want to be involved in the production," he told her firmly.

His tone made cinema sound like some criminal undertaking.

"But you'll be taking your cut," she pointed out, keeping her eye on him.

This man, she thought, is the laird.

If she handled this well and got him in the film, the boost to her own career would be significant.

They had reached a door.

"This is my tutorial," he explained.

She watched him as he rummaged for a key in a battered leather briefcase.

He looked up, apparently surprised to find her still there.

"Look, I'm not proud of my more commercial fiction," he admitted. "It was a spur-of-the-moment thing.

"I put pen to paper after reading some Walter Scott on a rainy day. My area of study is satirical poets of the eighteenth century.

"I don't usually enjoy the light-hearted or the popular."

"Something isn't poisonous because it's popular," she remarked.

He looked uncomfortable and for a moment their eyes met.

His were like dark amber, glowing behind his ridiculous round specs in the shadows of the cloister.

He turned away from her and unlocked the door, and Rosemary knew she had to leave.

But when she looked back a moment later, she saw some of his light brown hair.

He was still in the doorway, presumably checking that she was really going.

He was perfect for the part that Rosemary needed to fill.

He was aloof, snobby and patronising, just like the hero of the novel.

Even if he didn't turn out to have the acting ability of Peter O'Toole, he'd sound and look right.

And he'd written the book: cinema audiences would swoon over that connection.

This was priceless, and Rosemary was like a dog with a bone.

She hailed a passing student.

"Who's the boss of a professor?" she asked.

The boy looked startled.

"Golly. They're a law unto themselves, but the dean, I suppose."

"And where can I find the dean?"

The student gestured back towards the porter's lodge.

"First staircase by the chapel. Doctor Cross. He's nuts, but he's all right."

Doctor Cross was a tiny, timid man and Rosemary worked out

her strategy straightaway – a direct one that would send him into a tailspin.

Casually, she revealed Professor Randall's second identity as a romantic novelist and pulled from her bag the paperback edition.

Its colourful cover showed the laird, his clan tartan flying in the wind, his jaw square.

The heroine was in danger of falling out of her bodice and she was gazing up at him in open adoration.

Rosemary laid the copy on Dr Cross's desk and suggested that the college, an institution of refined learning, could do without this publicity.

"I imagine the professor has some academic publication on the horizon?" she said.

"Oh my goodness, yes – a whole book. Ground-breaking and a coup for the college."

"So I imagine that you'd prefer the professor to lie low for a bit, now that his side-line has been revealed?"

"Has it?" Dr Cross looked petrified.

"Nobody can keep this out of the press now," Rosemary carried on.

"Oh my goodness, what will the president say?"

"Kennedy?" Rosemary was surprised that news from Oxford colleges reached Washington DC.

"Boase, president of the college."

The expression on Dr Cross's face indicated that Boase was more important than God.

She gave Dr Cross a look of concerned anxiety.

"You wouldn't want newspapers crawling all over the quadrangles trying to interview him, would you?

"Magazines, too," she added, which made Dr Cross jump.

He asked if she had any suggestions and Rosemary considered the matter for a long time.

"Well," she finally said, "I am well placed to help, as luck would have it. I know his publisher, his agent – everybody.

"I could take the professor to London, for instance, and look after him for you."

Rosemary knew that Magdalen College would have even more of a problem if Randall ended up appearing in the film, but she'd cross that bridge when she came to it.

In her game, success was everything, and Rosemary was already imagining how her earnings would shoot up once her reputation was cemented.

Everyone who was anyone was holidaying abroad, and at her flat she had the details of a little place in the Balearics.

•   •   •   •

The college (probably its invisible president) "persuaded" Professor Randall that a short sabbatical would be a wise idea.

Soon he was installed in a respectable small hotel near Covent Garden, and his agent and publisher were "working on him".

Rosemary had queered her pitch – at least for a while – as the others were buttering him up before she went in for the kill.

They did a tremendous job, and before a fortnight was out, Rosemary was talking to a wary professor about the role and how wonderful it would be, "For you to seize this new challenge, Professor."

"I don't know how it would look to the college," he replied.

They were sitting opposite each other in the hotel lounge.

"I kept repeating that to your colleagues, but –"

"It's about progress, Professor Randall," Rosemary interrupted him. "Your other employers know it in their hearts that showing the college in a modern light is clever."

Rosemary was pleased with her phrase, "your other employers".

She was making him hers for the project, wrapping him up and adding a bow.

"Does Cambridge have a dashing film star on its staff?" she asked, driving the point home.

He blushed.

It looked charming, Rosemary thought – vulnerability in this handsome hunk – but it would have to be beaten out of him on set.

The laird in "The Daughter Of The Highlands" would never blush.

Finally Randall agreed to give it a try.

He told Rosemary that his book on 18th-century poets had gone to press, the term was at an end, and so he had some time on his hands.

"But don't use my real name," he told her. "Use Colin McDaniel for whatever publicity may be involved."

Whatever publicity, Rosemary thought with a secret smile.

He hasn't a clue.

There would be seven-feet-high posters, articles with his dreamy face at the top of them and probably even a few pieces something on television.

• • • •

Rosemary set to work.

The director she had chosen was young and able to take direction himself – a deliberate choice on Rosemary's part because this was her project.

Gently, she moved Randall into the role.

Diligently, she read the script with him, making sure he felt involved and consulted.

Carefully, she arranged screen tests with just him.

The actress playing opposite was a hard nut and might scare him off.

Rosemary tried in every way she could think of to mould her star.

She gave him all her time, taking him round London and then to the studios west of the city, introducing him to people who would flatter him and to other people who could be relied upon to fall in love with him.

She ran scenes in cosy restaurants to encourage him to "feel" the part, ran scenes in costume and out of it – scenes with tame actors who she knew would flatter him into giving a performance.

But Hugh Randall was terrible.

He knew every word of the script, but when he spoke them aloud they lay flat on the page like a rotten kipper.

By now Rosemary felt that she knew the man – his sense of humour, his particular vulnerabilities, his quirks.

It also meant that she could see the single, glaring hole in him:

he could not act.

She knew that she should be feeling icy panic about it, but the few weeks since he'd been with her, wandering London drinking endless tea and talking, had lulled her into a strange carelessness.

Rosemary felt almost as though her obsession with making "The Daughter Of The Highlands" a hit was falling away.

She had to buck up.

One morning a note was lying on Rosemary's desk when she got in.

"The professor dropped it off," Kitty told her. "Golly, my sister's boyfriend's cousin's friend was right. The man's gorgeous."

"Don't be ridiculous, Kitty," Rosemary said with unusual sharpness.

The note was short. Hugh felt that he was a failure and said he was fleeing back to Oxford.

The very substance of the ambitious is merely the shadow of a dream, he had written at the bottom. *"Hamlet", Act 2, Scene 2.*

Rosemary felt a constricting pain in her chest.

He often quoted Shakespeare, and a dozen other poets, too.

His conversation was like a garden with something new and colourful around every corner.

He also gave citations, because he knew where every line came from.

It astonished her.

Rosemary pushed the note into a drawer.

She was angry. But more than angry, she was disappointed.

There was something else, too, pushing at her heart.

She was sad.

"Golly, Rosemary, are you all right?"

Kitty was in the doorway, the kettle dangling from her hand.

"You look dreadful," she added.

"I'm fine," Rosemary replied. "You can go – I'm sure there's a bridalwear shop that needs you."

"It's ten in the morning." Kitty looked hurt.

"Oh yes, so it is. I'm sorry."

It was the film that was making her tetchy, Rosemary told herself.

The project's success was falling through her fingers like sand.

She might have to compromise and make something run-of-the-mill, with none of the glittering publicity she had dreamed of.

That was why she felt as though the blood was draining from her face.

That same day, a photograph appeared in the social pages of "The Mail".

It showed Rosemary coming out of a fashionable Soho restaurant on the arm of Professor Randall.

London's most glamorous couple take to the town! the headline read.

Rosemary stared at it, screwing up her eyes because it only took up a few column inches.

She was on his arm – in a way.

It had been wet out and she recalled leaning on him just as she felt as though she might slip.

There had been a few such moments of closeness, and now, sitting at her desk all alone, recalling them made Rosemary feel desolate.

The photograph had a bit of tabloid glamour about it.

She looked shapely in her sequin mini dress, her heavy bob

of ash blonde hair glinting under a street lamp.

He was splendid in an evening suit.

He was smiling a half smile and his dark good looks were cat-like and devastatingly attractive.

The evening papers used the same image, larger and more prominent.

Some fresh rumour or other about the novel and the film had caught the attention of journalists, and the photo was the perfect accompaniment.

Rosemary was in her flat when Hugh's agent called.

The jangle of the phone shocked her out of a reverie.

"You have to date him!" Janice's voice was shrill. "This is a better stunt than anything else you've achieved before!"

Janice was adamant that Hugh Randall's publisher had had the same thought.

"Forget the acting," Janice went on. "We've found out that he's hopeless. Now it's about you and a dishy gent from Oxford.

"Why did I not see this before? He's hot property, and so are you.

"Listen, Rosie, this film is going to be my 'Cleopatra', my 'Breakfast At Tiffany's', even if he's only the writer.

"He's the Arthur Miller to your Marilyn Monroe!"

Rosemary said she wasn't a Marilyn; she didn't act.

Janice verbally waved that away.

The film's producer called next, insisting that Rosemary needed to be photographed in Hugh's arms as soon as possible.

"I wish we'd spotted this sooner," he told her, "the star-maker and the star in love."

Irritably, Rosemary told him that Randall had returned to Oxford.

"Tempt him back, then. Wear that adorable dress from the photo." He paused. "You and I know that there's no need for it to last.

"A quick affair – even the appearance of a quick affair – and you'll be on the covers of magazines until the film opens.

"'Woman Of The Year' and 'Couple Of The Year'!"

"I'll have to call you back, Stephen," Rosemary replied. "I have a meeting."

There was no meeting, but Rosemary needed to think.

She shut the door of her office and stood in the centre of the room.

It was true – if she recast the laird's role, then keeping the attractive professor on the scene in some other way was the next best thing.

In fact, it might be preferable, because there was considerable risk in shoehorning a poor actor into a major role.

It was also true that a love affair between them would be gold dust for the movie.

The filmgoing public was fascinated by the inner workings of the industry.

They would make quite a couple – even Rosemary could see it.

Her day ahead, her week and the rest of her life – they seemed bleak now that he had gone.

She knew that she wanted him to come back, but could not bear the idea of manipulating him.

Rosemary had manipulated a

hundred people before – backers, actors, journalists and audiences.

She could manufacture almost anything, and often did.

But her blood was flowing down through her veins and arteries towards the floor.

She loved him.

This had crept up on her through all the frustrations and fatigue of trying to mould him into the laird.

She thought of him examining the iron fish wrapped round the lampposts along the Thames, or intrigued by the scenery flats at the Twickenham Studios, and longed, pure and simple, to see him again.

It scared her.

She had felt so safe with her solid bank balance and her notoriety.

The phone rang and automatically she picked it up.

"It's Professor Randall for you. Line one," Kitty announced.

If this was a final goodbye, it may as well come sooner rather than later.

She pressed the button.

"Did you get my note?" he asked.

His voice seemed distant, although the volume was high enough.

"Yes. Thank you."

There was nothing else she could say.

"I can't be in your film," he confirmed with her.

"No."

There was a silence.

Something was stopping him from ending the call. And why had he called in the first place?

"There's a conference on film," he went on. "Next term.

"It's not at Magdalen. The president's never been to a cinema as far as anyone knows."

The smile in his voice made her organs start to melt.

"I hope you can replace me," he added. "Well, obviously you can replace me.

"I mean that I hope you can replace me quickly and easily. I'm so sorry, Rosemary."

Rosemary sensed something between them – heat shooting across the miles of copper wire.

She had a choice at that moment, she realised.

She could take a risk or she could slide back into her old life.

It was a good life and secure.

But it was cold and slow and sad.

"You could just be the writer again," she suggested. "You could be Colin. You could even be anonymous if you want."

"But you'd know me," he replied.

His voice was smooth and deep and Rosemary felt cushioned in its folds.

"Yes, I do know you," she agreed.

"The film conference is too far off," he said. "It might not even interest you. Can I come back now? Would that be all right?"

"Please come back, whoever you are," she said.

"I didn't unpack, actually." He paused. "The film will be all right, won't it?"

"It will be a huge hit. The story is wonderful."

"All you need is a good love story," he replied.

And there it was again, the smile in his voice.

"That's all it takes."

My Favourite Photographs

My son, aged ten, in football gear,
(That it's brand new is very clear!);
My granddaughter, a sturdy two,
In ballet shoes and pink tutu!
Each page I turn brings memories
Of long-forgotten happy days.
It's not the same, scrolling a phone
(I hope in this I'm not alone) –
My hope is photographs will last
And not be relics of the past.

Eileen Hay

Illustration: Shutterstock.

GLEN DEVON, PERTHSHIRE

GLEN Devon is a place with special meaning for our cover feature writer, Willie Shand.
This steep-sided and dramatic cleft in the Ochils runs between Gleneagles and the fabulously named Yetts o'Muckhart.

Visitors will see drystone walls aplenty dividing up the grazing land – some of which were built by Willie's forebears.

Within easy reach of the bulk of Scotland's population in the Central Belt, the Ochils are fearsomely steep from the south and gentle sloping to the north. The reservoirs and woodlands here offer great walks amongst the rolling hills, as gentle or as strenuous as you'd like.

Accessible by good roads, it's been a particularly popular area for windfarm development.

We Meet Again

BY LYNNE HALLETT

PENNY for them."
Rachel jumped at the sound of Pete's voice as he walked into the kitchen.

"Sorry, love," he said. "I didn't mean to scare you."

"I know," she replied. "I was just thinking."

"Nice thoughts?"

"Not really. This came in the post."

She handed the piece of card to him.

He scanned it and raised an eyebrow.

"Your school reunion. Are you going to go?"

"I'm not sure."

She reached out to take the invitation back from him and stared at it again, as though it could provide an answer.

"I've spent years trying to forget about what happened. I don't think much is to be gained by going back. It would just be opening old wounds."

Her eyes pricked with tears, and she blinked them away before he could see.

"Maybe it would be a way of healing them once and for all, don't you think?" he replied. "Go and confront your demons, love. Isn't that what you tell all your clients to do?"

He sat down opposite her and reached across the table, taking her hand in his.

"I'll come with you, if you like, and if it's an invitation just for you, then I can sit in the car outside and read a book."

She looked up and smiled at him.

"I don't know what I did to deserve you."

Pete shook his head.

"Deserving doesn't come into it. We were meant to be together. I'll make you a cuppa. It might help you decide."

Rachel continued to turn over the invitation between her fingers, before placing it down on the table in front of her.

You are cordially invited to the Chesterleigh High School reunion, class of 1988, on March 15, 7.00-10 p.m.

To be held in the main hall. Buffet and disco.

Please RSVP to L. Thompson.

She furrowed her brow. She couldn't remember an L. Thompson.

Illustration by Martin Baines.

But that didn't mean much. It could be any one of the Louises or Lorraines or Lindas she had been at school with, who had got married.

Her stomach somersaulted and she could feel her mind spinning like a top.

She took a deep breath to calm her nerves and reached for the tea as Pete brought it over.

"I've put more sugar in than usual." He smiled again. "I'd better get back to the study, Rach. You know where I am if you need me."

"Thanks. I think I just need to busy myself and forget all about this invitation for a while."

"Good plan."

Pete bent down and kissed the top of her head before leaving the kitchen.

Rachel sipped her tea and tried unsuccessfully to block out scenes from her past.

She screwed up her eyes tightly, but still she saw it all playing out in front of her as if on a loop.

She thought she'd dealt with this and come to terms with what happened, but it seemed she was wrong.

• • • •

"How are you this morning?" ➤

Pete turned to look at Rachel.

"I didn't sleep that well, to be honest." That was an understatement.

She'd struggled to drop off, and then when she had, her sleep was fitful, full of the sorts of dreams that made no sense but contained that hint of threat.

A typical anxiety dream. Her clients told her about those all the time.

Pete yawned.

"I know."

"I'm sorry," she told him. "Did I keep you awake?"

"Maybe just a bit. At least it's a weekend so I can take it easy."

She moved in and kissed him.

"You stay in bed. I think I'll go for a run to clear my mind."

"It sounds like a good idea. You take care."

He turned over, pulled the duvet up and she got out of bed.

Half an hour later she was ready to leave.

The cold air was like a slap in the face.

It might be spring, but there was still a hint of winter in the air.

At least it wasn't raining, though.

She started off at a gentle pace to warm up, pounding the tarmac and heading for the hills, listening to her running playlist, full of power songs with a strong rhythm.

She tried to empty her mind and just focus on her breathing and putting one foot in front of another, fully getting into her stride within minutes.

She liked the discipline of running and the way it helped her to just live in the moment rather than the past.

It was one of her coping strategies, and it was healthier than some other things that people turned to in order to block out their troubles.

As she ran up the hill, all her focus was on reaching the summit.

When she did, her heart was pounding and she was a little out of breath, but the beautiful view was her reward.

She stood, her hands on hips, taking it all in, enjoying as she always did seeing the town from on high, picking out landmarks, including the Priory where she and Pete had been married.

She smiled instinctively as she thought of her husband.

Pete, her one true love, the one who kept her grounded.

She considered what he had said yesterday.

Her eyes landed on the local comprehensive, the campus sprawled out beneath her.

Her school days hadn't been the happiest days of her life.

She sat down on a rock and thought about the invitation to the reunion.

It was a clear decision of go or don't go. If she chose not to go, then life would carry on much the same.

She could stuff the bad memories back into their box, lock the lid and forget about them. Well, sort of.

If she chose to go, then maybe she would be standing up for herself in a way she hadn't at the time.

Of course, there was every chance she would see the girl who had caused her unhappiness, teased her and verbally bullied her.

Her stomach somersaulted again. She was still frightened, and it wasn't a good feeling.

But, she reasoned, there was no way anyone would behave like that at a reunion, especially not as an adult.

And she could leave if there was any nastiness.

If she could just pull herself together and attend, she might get some answers and be able to make sense of what had happened.

• • • •

"How do I look?" Rachel stood and did a twirl, acting more confident than she felt.

"Amazing. But then you always look amazing." Pete's smile always made her melt.

She smoothed the skirt of her dress down.

She was wearing a black dress, high heels, a pearl necklace and earrings, and she had applied make-up a touch more dramatically than her usual daytime look.

"I'll be surprised if they even recognise you," he added.

She giggled.

"You could be right. I don't look anything like I did then."

"And you're not like you were then, either. Remember, you are strong and confident now."

"Yes, I am."

Rachel followed Pete to the car and, once inside, leaned back as he drove her to the reunion.

Her old school was a good hour's drive from their home, and she leaned back, letting the soothing tones of a selection of crooners wash over her.

Pete didn't tend to talk much when he was driving, far preferring to concentrate on the road.

It seemed like no time at all until he was pulling into the school car park.

The school looked vaguely as she remembered it, but the main building had been extended and it appeared less worn than it had in her day.

She gulped and then exhaled.

Pete reached out and patted her thigh.

"You've got this, Rach."

She turned to him, her eyes wide.

"I wish I had your confidence."

"Fake it till you make it. I have a feeling you're going to be pleasantly surprised."

"I hope you're right." Her voice quavered slightly. "OK, I'm going."

Rachel opened the car door, swung her legs out, shut it a little harder than she intended and approached the main entrance.

The doors still had those sturdy handles that you had to pull, but the entrance itself had been revamped.

No-one was around, but there was a board in front of her, propped up and filled with school photos from her year group.

She cast her eyes over the faces in front of her, all young, fresh and, in some cases, spotty.

She found her own photo and felt a momentary sadness for that sixteen-year-old girl, who was a little plump, bespectacled, brace-ridden and with hair in need of styling.

Add to that the fact that she

was clever, and she could see why she was prime bullying material.

Her eyes ranged around the board looking for Claire, and her mouth gaped.

Someone had taken a red marker pen to it, added devil's horns, glasses, a moustache and a goatee.

Maybe people weren't as grown up in their fifties as she thought they might be.

Rachel believed she'd come off worst in terms of being bullied, but Claire had cast her net wide.

How would she feel when she saw that?

How would she be able to show her face?

"Hello, there. May I take your name?"

She turned towards a woman holding a clipboard.

She was small, round and smiley.

Maybe this was L. Thompson?

She searched her face but couldn't recognise her.

"Oh, yes. It's Rachel Jefferson. Well, Rachel Harris. And you are?"

"Oh, wow! Rachel? You look fab!

"It's Louise. Louise Barker, as was." Louise lowered the clipboard and pointed to a sticker on her dress.

"Louise?" Rachel tried to disguise her shock.

Louise had been so petite and fragile as a teenager.

"I know. We've all changed a lot, haven't we?" She nodded in the direction of the main hall.

"I love your dress. It really suits you," Rachel told her kindly.

Louise had been one of the nicer girls, even if she hadn't been a friend as such.

Louise's blush deepened.

"I could say the same for you," she replied. "You'll have to share your secret with me later. You look great!

"Anyway, take this sticker and then everyone will know who you are."

Rachel reached out for the sticker, putting it on her dress.

She wasn't quite sure who she was in this situation.

Not the Rachel she had been, by any stretch of the imagination, but back in her old school she could feel aspects of the old Rachel stirring.

She would have preferred anonymity.

Perhaps she could take her sticker off when she was inside and remain an enigma to most of the attendees.

Uncertain of how to proceed, Rachel just smiled again.

"I guess I'll head off to the hall, then. See who else I can find."

Or avoid, she thought.

She hesitated for a moment.

"Is . . ." She couldn't bring herself to ask. "No, don't worry. I'll find out for myself."

Louise stared at her.

"You want to know if Claire's here, don't you?"

It was her turn to redden now. Best just to confess.

"It might be useful to know."

Louise's expression softened.

"She is. But she's changed, too. She was all set to dart out when she saw that." She pointed at the picture. "I encouraged her to stay.

"But I'm not sure she'll be here for long. She hadn't taken her coat off when I left the hall."

"Well, that is a turn up for the

books."

Rachel frowned slightly and followed the arrows to the hall, not that she needed to be reminded of how to get there, even after all this time.

As she entered, a smile came to her face, in spite of her worries.

It had been beautifully decorated.

There were balloons and a massive banner reminding them of when they had left.

The stage had a microphone on it ready for the introductions later on, she assumed, and a projector screen lay behind.

Most likely they would be shown a plethora of photos; they hadn't really ever been filmed, as far as she could remember.

There was a long table along one side of the room, bearing a buffet, and round tables covered in crisp white cloths were dotted around.

There was ample space in the middle for dancing, though no-one was dancing yet, despite some Eighties hits playing in the background.

After taking in the room, her eyes sought out familiar faces, though those who had arrived already were forming small groups and all she could see was the backs of their heads.

Maybe she would seek out Claire first.

She glanced around and saw a woman sitting alone in the furthest corner of the room, clutching a drink, still wearing her coat.

That had to be her, though from this distance she wouldn't necessarily have recognised her.

Taking a deep, calming breath,

Rachel strode purposefully towards the table, aware that while her heart was beating quicker, the fear that had gripped her as a teenager was no longer there. That surprised her.

"May I join you?" she asked when she got closer.

"Feel free. I'm not staying anyway."

"It's Claire, isn't it? Claire Sanders?"

Claire's eyes widened.

"How do you know?"

"Well, the badge does rather give it away." She smiled as Claire rolled her eyes. "Though I must say you look very much the same as you did back then."

"Do you think so?"

"Yes." She looked less brash, though, and less confident.

"I'm afraid I don't recognise you. Where's your sticker?"

"Oh, my jacket is covering it. I'm Rachel."

She removed her jacket and stared at Claire, watching the emotions move over her face.

Shock registered first and her mouth gaped, and then something else.

Was it guilt or embarrassment? Claire looked down at her drink, breaking eye contact.

She seemed to have retreated even further into herself and become even smaller.

After a few seconds she looked up.

"I would have thought you'd want to avoid me."

Rachel pulled out a chair and sat opposite Claire.

"I did. And then I thought that maybe seeing you would be good for me."

"Good for you?" Claire

repeated.

"Well, things were never really resolved, were they? We left school and that was it," Rachel replied. "But I didn't quite leave what had happened behind."

She kept her eyes fixed on Claire, taking in all the subtle changes and movements that would allow her to make a professional interpretation of how her former adversary was feeling.

Claire looked decidedly as if she wanted to bolt to get out of this awkward situation, but she was cornered.

She raised her glass and downed the remains of her drink.

Rachel felt herself growing stronger by the minute.

"Can I just ask you one thing?" Rachel began.

Claire nodded.

There was a silence. When Claire spoke again, her voice was quiet.

"I'm not proud of how I behaved back then to the people around me, especially you," she admitted. "It came home to me tonight just how much everyone must hate me – or at least someone still does."

"You mean the photo?" Rachel replied.

"Yes. I half wondered if you were responsible for the artwork. But as you seem to have arrived after me, it must have been someone else.

"I guess it doesn't matter who. The fact someone would deface my photo speaks volumes."

Rachel's heart twinged ever so slightly.

Surely she wasn't feeling sorry for Claire?

"I wasn't sure about coming. I thought I'd leave the past in the past and all that," Claire went on. "I'm nothing like I was then, though I guess that might be hard to believe.

"But my husband suggested it would be an opportunity to make amends."

Rachel smiled.

"My husband persuaded me, too. He said I might achieve closure."

"Husbands, eh?" Claire attempted a smile, but it vanished quickly.

She paused.

"You really want to know why I bullied you?"

"Yes, I do," Rachel insisted.

"Because I was jealous of you. How pathetic is that?" She put her head in her hands for a moment, before looking up again. "I'm so sorry.

"I know that an apology after thirty years will probably be pointless, but I want you to hear it all the same.

"I have no excuses as to why I did it. But you . . . you seemed to have it all. I wanted to be top of the class, but every time I tried harder, so did you.

"I wanted to be the best, but I never was. And everyone liked you," Claire continued. "There was just something so lovely about you that it . . . aggravated me."

Rachel sat quietly, absorbing what she had heard, not wanting to interrupt.

Claire carried on.

"I didn't carry on behaving like that. Not when I left school. Honestly, I didn't. But by the time I saw the error of my ways, it was too late to do anything about it.

"I couldn't make amends to you and the others, but I decided that I would be a better person and try to help people in my career."

"What do you do?" Rachel's curiosity was piqued.

"I joined the police force. I thought catching criminals and protecting the innocent would absolve me of my sins." Claire shrugged.

"And has it?" Rachel asked. She nodded.

"To some extent. But I've carried the guilt around with me and I'm always going to be remembered as the school bully by you lot."

She gestured to the others in the room.

"Well, I can't speak for everyone else, but I might just be able to change my opinion of you now." Rachel smiled encouragingly.

"You're just saying that."

"No, I'm not. It seems like we have more in common than I thought."

"Seriously?" Claire raised an eyebrow.

Rachel nodded.

"Well, for a start we both came here even though we had reservations. Secondly, I chose a career linked to my experiences, too.

"I'm a therapist and life coach. I specialise in helping people get over trauma.

"It's ironic that I manage to sort everyone else out but not myself. I am very bad at following my own advice."

Claire cleared her throat before replying.

"So what would you advise me to do, professionally speaking, if I were one of your clients?" she asked Rachel.

"I think you've just done it." Rachel smiled warmly and it felt natural to do so. "I accept your apology and I am grateful for the explanation. We're all works in progress, especially when we're young.

"We shouldn't be judged by who we were then or what we did. We've both come a long way."

"Thank you, Rachel. You're very generous. More generous than I deserve." Tears filled Claire's eyes and she blinked them away.

"Look, if I can forgive you, I think you can forgive yourself," Rachel pointed out. "We can't turn the clock back, but there's no point carrying that guilt around a moment longer.

"How about you take your coat off and I'll get us both another drink. Then we can try mingling, if you feel up to it, or dancing when the music gets going."

"I'd like that." Claire smiled for the first time. "At least, I think so. I haven't been to a disco in years."

Rachel walked over to the buffet table and picked up two glasses of wine.

Pete had been right, though even he couldn't have foreseen that she would end up socialising with the one person she had dreaded seeing.

Life was full of surprises, that was for sure, and she felt that it might be just that bit better for her and Claire after tonight. ◼

Hope Springs Eternal

BY BAILEY MORGAN

MUMMY!"
The yell set my heart thundering.
I thought my little one must have hurt herself, fallen on the patio and scraped her knees.

I charged out of the kitchen and found her pointing to a bucket that Sam, her dad, had abandoned on the slabs.

He'd started building a new garden wall weeks ago and had left behind a blue tarpaulin, a bag of concrete mix, a pile of sand and various buckets collecting rainwater.

Inside the murky depths of one bucket, its wings spread, lay a motionless small brown bird.

Judging by a dusty imprint on the lounge window, it must have hit the glass then fell, unconscious, to its doom.

"Mummy, help it!"

My four-year-old possessed no concept of the impossible.

At that moment I didn't have one, either.

I scooped up the bird, carefully folding in its drenched wings.

Even wet it weighed nothing at all. It felt like a cold cloud in my palms.

"You need to wrap it up, then it'll get better," my daughter instructed me.

She'd reached the stage where she liked to tell me what to do.

She'd choose her clothes in the morning.

"I'll wear the blue dress, Mummy."

She'd pick out all the meals she could, too.

"I'll have fish fingers for lunch, please."

I might have said it was far too late for the bird.

But, staring down into her wide blue eyes, I remembered far too clearly that, left to her own devices, she wouldn't have survived, either.

I did wonder later if some hidden instinct took over when I went running into the kitchen and grabbed a tea towel to dry off the bird.

I wrapped it in some kitchen roll next to further soak up the moisture.

Then I hunted for a box.

I found one under the stairs. I tipped out a pair of new trainers and replaced them with my soggy patient.

I closed the lid after puncturing

Illustration by Shutterstock.

in some air holes.

"That's good, Mum," I was told with a nod of approval as I set the box on a shelf close to a radiator.

There, the heat would warm it through.

My daughter had needed warmth as well.

Born at twenty-nine weeks, she'd spent months in an incubator.

Unable to hold her straightaway, I cuddled a vast assortment of soft toys – a teddy, a fluffy cat, a rabbit with over-sized ears.

Lingering by my little one's fish tank of a bed, I sang her lullabies, awestruck by how anyone so fragile could cling on to life so doggedly.

Still, her doctors had only given her a fifty-fifty chance of survival due to her severely undeveloped lungs.

"It'll get better now," she said in the kitchen.

OK, the day felt blighted. It would likely never fly again.

"Right, then, what were we going to do this afternoon?"

"Planting?"

"Planting. Yes, planting."

Sam, in his efforts to make the garden look less of a waste ground, had purchased lots of pots and plants.

Since the warm weather was ➤

waning, he'd picked pansies to bloom over the autumn and winter.

Under the lounge window, they stood in tray after tray, row after row.

I think the garden centre must have a special offer on.

"Let's get cracking, then."

Outside, I pondered as we toiled, wrapped up in our coats, the potting compost sticking to our chilly fingers.

I needed to find a positive way out of this bird situation.

I needed to handle things gently in a manner that a four-year-old could grasp.

Only not yet . . .

"I'm not ready," I'd said the same in the hospital many times in the neonatal suite, unwilling to leave.

I harboured a notion that, if I walked away, my precious scrap of life would stop breathing.

Sam would tug at my hand as I stood rooted.

"You need to get some rest, Lisa."

He'd booked us into a nearby hotel for the duration.

He'd taken paternity leave, planning to take holiday leave on top if necessary.

I hadn't even rung the office where I worked to update them.

Too lost in the moment, I'd simply left Sam to handle it all.

I'd leaned on him so hard, but he'd coped magnificently.

Still, even a mighty oak can crack.

Sometimes his voice would gain an edge, the waiting so wearying.

We'd do next to nothing all day yet feel exhausted. Every hour brimmed with doubt.

Maybe or maybe not, our baby's lungs would grow.

Perhaps, instead, an infection would steal her away in a moment.

I really needed Sam again now.

"You carry on. Mummy's just going to go down to the apple tree and check for moles."

Moles? Sometimes I wonder where my ideas come from.

I pulled my phone out of my pocket and dialled as I walked away.

When Sam answered my call in his office, I explained in hushed tones, watching our daughter pat down the soil again under our pansies as if she wanted to give them every chance to thrive.

"Is she too young for all this?" I asked my husband after I've passed on the gist of things. "I think it's a sparrow. I don't think it's alive.

"I need to bury it, don't I?"

He didn't reply.

"Sam? Sam? Hello?" I called.

"Could you give it another half an hour?" he said finally.

"You mean make an appointment for its demise?"

"Why not? I know, give it until four, then give her 'the talk'."

"What is 'the talk?'"

He paused again.

"Something age-appropriate?"

I let out a slow breath, tears prickling my eyes.

I wasn't prepared.

"Are you all right?" he asked.

"No, I'm not."

"Do you want to wait until I come home? I'll get back as fast as I can and we can do it together."

"Good idea," I agreed.

We're a team. We've survived

far worse.

Indeed, our baby's heart stopped one morning.

It happened after weeks of improvements.

The nurses came charging over to her unit, alerted by a long, low beep.

They crowded in, nudging Sam and me back, a doctor pushing to the fore.

My memory's a bit hazy of what happened afterwards.

I do recall calls for this and that, the jargon beyond me, medical things injected into lines.

Then suddenly I was floating. I'm sure my feet left the tiles.

I drifted upwards as if, as my baby left the world, I would be gifted a last goodbye somewhere near the strip-light or by a big dent in the false ceiling.

Then Sam shook me and spoke words into my face I couldn't comprehend.

"They've got her back. It's OK." Then he crushed me to his chest.

Don't you ever do that again, I told our baby in my head. Promise me.

I'd tensed, waiting and waiting for her to defy instructions.

I will go away, Mummy. I'm too delicate for this world.

• • • •

In the garden we planted more pansies: a forest of purple, yellow and maroon.

Every once in a while I was asked about the bird.

I didn't go and check.

I told her that it was in shock and needed lots of rest.

"Little birds take their time," I added.

The minutes limped onwards.

Sam would rush home, I knew it.

He'd drive at the edge of the speed limit all the way.

He'd tap impatiently at his steering wheel if the traffic snarled up on the motorway.

He'd sit waiting for a miracle.

Oh Sam. You silly, silly man . . .

Finally, about five-thirty, as we stood in the kitchen, drinking down milk or, in my case, a big mug of tea, the front door opened and in he strode, tie askew, his bag swinging.

"Daddy!" the usual chorus welcomed him.

He scooped up our baby and held her tight, closed his eyes and hung on.

He always does the same.

Letting go, finally he came over and kissed my cheek.

"How's the patient?" he whispered.

I shook my head and motioned towards the box on its shelf.

"It's not made a sound," I replied.

"I see." He sighed, then crouched down one more time. "Sweetheart, we're not sure the birdie will wake up."

Had he Googled it at work, hunting for the best way to explain?

Would he make a sweet little speech that he had rehearsed while articulated lorries made his car wobble as they passed him on the duel carriageway?

I closed my eyes, giddy with it all – only that's as far as he got.

"Come and help Daddy."

He took our little one's hand and led her away.

I wiped at my eyes and tried to pull myself together.

➤

I really didn't want to handle the matter at all as memories swirled.

The first day I'd held our daughter, I looked down at her face as she lay in my arms, still attached to so many tubes and wires.

I imagined the day she would feed.

I frowned then, thinking of myself as some kind of mystical, magical creature out of a very weird volume of "Harry Potter".

I was a life-giver twice over.

I wouldn't only nourish her. My antibodies would protect her with every greedy gulp.

She did gulp, but not for weeks more.

She gulped and gulped and grew stronger and stronger.

"I am a giver of life," I said to myself in the kitchen loftily. "Oh, come on, birdie, do you hear me? I've tried a tea towel and some kitchen roll.

"Give me a break, will you? It's a lovely day. I don't want it ruined."

Selfish, I know.

I walked outside.

Down the garden I went, over to Sam.

He'd chosen a spot under the apple tree to point out a few bugs, a ladybird, and a black crawling beetle.

I crouched down and held out my arms.

"I need a hug. Hope?"

That's what we'd christened our little one – Hope.

"OK, Mummy." Hope held on to me, careful not to crush me with her enthusiasm.

It might seem like madness, but my girl at birth was only around 37 centimetres long.

She could just about fit across her daddy's palms.

The bird was even smaller.

As she released me, Hope smiled.

"Can we see how the birdie is now?"

Her question felt like a stray mosquito crawling across my back.

I then shared a glance with her dad.

"Er, well . . ."

He turned ashen as we both gazed back down the lawn.

Now I know my tale can end only one of two ways. That's life and death for you.

Many would add a sprinkle of common sense, too, and say, "I'm afraid, the odds aren't high".

Still, I walked down the bright green grass hand in hand with my husband and our little one.

Together we fetched the shoebox.

We placed it in the middle of the lawn.

"Please, please be all right, little bird."

I removed the lid and dared to peer inside.

I had met a delicate creature once before with a tenacious grip on life.

I met one more as the sparrow shook out its feathers.

Miracles do happen, you see. They happen every day.

If you're still a cynic, then here's my advice: take a moment to marvel at the wonder in a child's eyes.

I wish that I could say I saw the bird take flight, but I only gazed at Hope as it reclaimed the skies. ■

TRIM THE CAT

TRIM, a ship's cat with an extraordinary tale, sailed alongside Matthew Flinders on his historic voyage to circumnavigate Australia.

Born aboard *HMS Reliance*, Trim's adventurous spirit and intelligence endeared him to the crew. He braved treacherous seas, shipwreck and even imprisonment with Matthew in Mauritius. Sadly, Trim disappeared during their captivity, leaving the seafarer heartbroken.

Today, a bronze statue of Trim stands alongside Matthew's statue in Sydney's Mitchell Library.

Trim's legacy lives on, with another statue dedicated to him at Port Lincoln in South Australia, and yet another outside Euston Station in London.

Image: Wikimedia Commons.

A Scottish Summer

BY HILARY SPIERS

ELAINE pulled back the curtain a fraction to get a better view of the street. Two men in polo shirts were leaning against the side of the removal lorry having a smoke.

"Cold drink, lads?" a female voice called but, try as she might, Elaine couldn't see its owner.

Definitely an English accent, though.

The men hastily stubbed out their cigarettes and disappeared from view, returning to their station moments later with a glass each.

"Cheers!" one of them shouted, raising the glass in a toast, and there was an answering laugh from the woman.

"I've got to keep you hydrated, haven't I? We would have to choose the hottest day of the year to move! I wasn't expecting the weather to be like this. Everyone said it would be raining all the time.

"But you're doing a marvellous job. I'm in the kitchen if you need me."

The men knocked back their drinks, placed the empty glasses on the low stone wall and climbed back inside the removal van.

Elaine waited a few minutes to see what they brought out next, but then she spotted Ailsa across the road looking directly at her and she drew back guiltily.

She would hate to be accused of snooping, so she went back to her crossword.

She had been curious about her new neighbours ever since the *Sold* notice had gone up, hoping that the newcomers would inject a bit of life into their quiet community.

It seemed like ages since they'd heard young voices or watched children playing.

She thought with a sharp pang of her son and his family far away in New Zealand.

Their weekly catch-ups on FaceTime were a blessing, but there was nothing like the feel of her grandchildren's arms around her, their vitality and joy . . .

She berated herself. She was getting maudlin. She'd see them at Christmas.

But Christmas was months away.

Fifteen minutes later she looked out of the window again to check the weather.

She needed a few things at the shop. Or so she told herself.

Illustration: Shutterstock.

In truth, it was simply an excuse to get out of the house and stretch her legs.

The sky, blue no longer, was now grey and forbidding with scudding clouds, and a sharp wind had sprung up.

She went through to the hall and shrugged on her hooded raincoat.

No point taking an umbrella: it would be blown inside-out in seconds.

She picked up her shopping bag and purse and headed out just as it started to drizzle.

The removal men were scurrying into the house next door with a couple of chairs apiece.

She waited to allow them to cross the pavement in front of her.

"Thanks, missus!" one of them shouted. "What's happened to the sun? It's freezin' all of a sudden."

Elaine laughed and called after them as they reached the doorway.

"That's Scotland for you! Sunny and dreich all in a day."

The men disappeared and Elaine went to move on, only to be hailed by a figure in the doorway.

"Hello!"

A woman stood on the front step, huddled into an oversized cardigan, frowning up at the sky.

"We're just moving in. Do you ➤

live around here?"

Elaine tugged her hood further over her forehead, grimacing as the drizzle turned to proper rain.

"Next door. Welcome to the street. Let me know if there's anything you need."

"Oh," the woman replied. "That's very kind of you."

She stepped back as rain splashed on to the doorstep.

"But please don't let me keep you. You're getting soaked."

"Ach, a wee bit rain won't kill me." Elaine said. "I'm no' made of sugar."

The woman laughed warmly.

She raised a hand to bid farewell, then paused just as Elaine was about to move on.

"Unless you'd like to pop in for a quick cuppa?"

Elaine was taken aback. She had never been inside 32, Leven Crescent in all the 20-odd years Craig McDougall had lived there.

He had made keeping himself to himself into a fine art.

It had taken Elaine and Angus nearly five years to get a greeting out of him.

Their repeated attempts to get to know him had been so firmly rebuffed that they had soon given up.

No-one else in the street had had much to do with the man whom Elaine had always thought must be terribly lonely.

And now she knew how that felt.

"Well, if you're sure . . ."

Seconds later she was shedding her rain-sodden coat and being ushered past countless large, cardboard boxes in the hall, through into the kitchen, where a small pine table and two chairs sat amid a mountain of tea chests.

Her hostess held out a hand.

"Lucy Carter. Lovely to meet you."

Elaine took her hand.

"Och, pet, you're that cold! I'm Elaine Baird."

"It was sunny when we arrived," Lucy said, shivering. "Now look at it! Thank heavens I'd just unpacked David's jumpers.

"This is his, in case you were wondering."

She dropped her arms to her sides and the sleeves fell almost to her knees.

Both women laughed.

"This'll blow through," Elaine said as Lucy made for the sink with the kettle.

"Will it? It looks like it's set in for the day," Lucy replied.

"Forecast said rain at three, blue skies by four. Just keep your cardi handy, that's my advice," Elaine added.

Overhead came the sound of children's voices, followed by the thunder of feet on the stairs.

The kitchen door burst open and two small girls in T-shirts and shorts came to an abrupt halt as they saw the stranger in front of them.

"Hello," Elaine said, beaming. "I live next door. My name's Elaine."

"Mrs Baird to you," Lucy said.

"No, please, Elaine's fine."

"Well, this is Ruby and Amelia," Lucy said, pointing at each girl in turn. "Girls, say hello to Elaine."

"Hello," the pair chorused dutifully. "Mum, we're starving. And we're so cold!"

Lucy looked round the kitchen distractedly.

"I thought I brought a carrier in here with biscuits and some fruit, but I can't put my hands on it."

The girls groaned.

"Pop up and get your coats if you're cold," Lucy told them. "I'll find you warmer clothes in a bit."

Elaine got to her feet.

"Lucy, I best get on my way. You've enough on your plate. We can have tea another time. I was just going to the shops, so why don't I pick up some things for the girls?"

"No, I couldn't possibly –" Lucy started, just as Ruby and Amelia shouted, "Yes, please!"

"There," Elaine said. "That's settled. What would you like?"

The girls exchanged uncertain looks.

"Do you have Penguins up here?" Ruby asked.

Elaine laughed.

"We most certainly do! And Empire biscuits, Tunnock's tea cakes, shortbread, tablet and clootie dumplings . . ."

The girls frowned.

"Clootie what?" Amelia asked.

"You'll see." Elaine smiled.

Ruby looked dubious.

"I think we should come and look for ourselves. You might choose things we don't like."

"Ruby!" Lucy looked mortified. "Don't be so cheeky! Elaine, I do apologise."

"No need; I was only teasing. Girls, if your mother allows, I'd be delighted to have you come along with me. Then you can pick exactly what you'd like.

"May I, Lucy?"

So five minutes later, Elaine and the two girls, bundled up in jackets and scarves but still in their shorts, climbed the hill to the shop, leaving Lucy to supervise the removal men and search myriad boxes for the missing supplies.

She had tried to press some notes on Elaine, which had been roundly rejected.

"Think of it as a house-warming present," Elaine had told her. "My pleasure."

By the time they emerged on to the street again, laden with biscuits, crisps and sweets, plus a hand of bananas and a bag of apples, the rain had stopped, the wind had dropped and the sun had re-emerged.

Soon the girls had shed their outer garments (which Elaine found herself carrying) and were skipping down the crescent swinging the shopping bag between them.

Elaine hugged the jackets and scarves to her, memories of other jackets, other girls, suddenly assailing her.

Back at the house, the removal men were still unloading the lorry and, in the kitchen, Lucy continued her fruitless search for the missing carrier.

"It's ridiculous!" she exclaimed to Elaine, "I labelled everything so carefully! Well, David did."

Where, Elaine wondered, was David?

As if reading her thoughts, Lucy replied.

"I expect you're wondering why my husband isn't here. He's stuck down in London finishing a project. Last-minute crisis. Everything was booked, so we decided the girls and I would come on up here as planned to get the girls settled into school for the new term and all that.

"My intention was to have everything sorted by the ➤

weekend, when he gets here. Fat chance of that.

"Girls, don't eat all those biscuits!" she admonished her daughters. "We'll be having supper in an hour or so."

"What are we having?" Amelia asked, sliding a packet of crisps out of her mother's sight.

Elaine suppressed a smile.

Lucy's face fell.

"Well, if I can just find the box with the tins and utensils . . . it must be here somewhere."

She caught Elaine's eye.

"You must think I'm hopeless!"

"Not at all. Moving's no picnic at the best of times. Nothing's ever where you expect it to be."

"Could we have fish and chips?" Ruby asked. "Please, Mum!"

Lucy looked at her neighbour questioningly.

Elaine shook her head.

"The van only comes on a Tuesday."

"The van?"

"Aye, Gordon shut the chippie last year and now he has a wee van that tours around the area. But he's only here once a week."

"Sorry, girls," Lucy said, deflated.

The girls sighed.

A thought struck Elaine. She didn't want to appear pushy, but her heart went out to her new neighbours, strangers in a new town in a new country.

"Would it help if you came round to me for your tea? Your supper?" she asked, hastily clarifying. "Just while you're catching your breath and finding your feet? "

"Can we, Mum?" Amelia said eagerly.

"Girls, it's very kind of Elaine to offer, but I'm sure she has enough to do getting a meal ready for her own family . . ."

"Angus, my husband, died six months ago," Elaine said quietly. "And I can't tell you how much I miss cooking for someone and sharing a meal with them.

"It would give me so much pleasure to help you out, if you'd like that. But please, don't feel obliged."

"Obliged?" Lucy repeated, with a tiny crack in her voice. "I'm overwhelmed. If I'm honest, I've been dreading this move. We're only here because of David's work.

"I didn't know what to expect – certainly not for someone I've only just met to be so kind and generous."

"Please," Elaine said, feeling embarrassed. "I'll take that as a yes, hen.

"Why don't the girls pop round with me now and see what they would like. You let me know when the men have finished unloading and we'll eat once you're free."

She glanced out of the window, her mind already running through the contents of her larder and freezer.

She thought she might hold back on the haggis and the Cullen skink until she knew her neighbours and their tastes better.

"In fact, if the weather holds, we might eat out on the patio. It'll not be dark until about eleven."

"Eleven?" Lucy was astonished, as the girls whooped with delight.

"Aye. Four seasons in a day, pet. And long summer nights. It makes up for our winters.

"Welcome to Scotland." ∎

Illustration: Shutterstock.

Putting Down Roots

BY SHEELAGH MOONEY

AILISH stretched her arms out in pleasure. Not for the first time she considered how lucky she was to have moved here.

She loved this old rectory with its rambling gardens and orchard. She and her husband Hugo had moved here after she had taken redundancy from her job.

Working as an illustrator for a publishing company in the city, she'd saved up enough to make it possible to live in this tiny village.

It was as far from her former existence as it was possible to be.

"I'm off now. You won't be lonely, will you? You're more than welcome to come with me!" Hugo called from the hallway.

"I know, Hugo, but I'm much happier pottering in the garden here than staying in a hotel somewhere. Especially when you'll be working every minute of every hour."

"You're probably right. You love this old place, don't you?"

"I do, Hugo. The more time I spend in it, the more I love it.

"Remember to give me a call

when you arrive just to let me know you got there safely!"

Hugo smiled, assured her he would, kissed her cheek and headed for the door.

"Will do, my love. I'll see you Friday, Allie, all going well."

Ailish waved him off then closed the door with a sigh.

As much as she loved Hugo, she hadn't left her job to spend her time trailing around the world after him. It was still a novelty to be a free agent and she was enjoying every last minute of it.

There was a lot of work involved in the restoration of the garden to its past glory.

Unbeknownst to Hugo, she rather appreciated the weeks when he was away for work. The days stretched out before her and she could do as she pleased.

Sometimes she did a bit of painting or writing, but more often she worked in the garden long into the evenings.

She looked at the breakfast dishes on the table and quickly piled them into the dishwasher.

Ailish did not intend to spend one minute longer than was necessary on housework. She planned to spend the week in the garden and only return to the house when hunger or bed beckoned her in.

The garden was both her canvas and her blank page, and she could hardly wait to give it her undivided attention.

She picked up her garden gloves, hat and secateurs and headed out the back.

In no time she was immersed in a world of her own, only semi-conscious of the cacophony of birdsong in the background.

She worked happily until afternoon, reclaiming the existing flower-beds, weeding, edging beds and pruning as she went.

She was thrilled to unearth some rare plant gems among the rough tangle of shrubs and bushes.

"Hello! Allie, are you in there?" A voice called out.

Ailish sat back from her digging.

"Look at this place! You've turned it into a regular paradise already," Clodagh, her sister, appeared through the shrubs.

Clodagh had never donned a pair of gardening gloves in her life, and her gardening knowledge didn't stretch further than having seen a few episodes of "Gardeners' World".

She was wearing a large straw hat, a stylish floral dress and tiny strappy sandals on her feet.

"Clodagh, what a nice surprise! What brings you to these parts?"

"You, of course! I came for the grand tour. It looks fabulous from the outside. I brought chocolate eclairs from the village bakery. I knew it would take something special to tempt you away from the garden on a day like this."

Allie smiled. Clodagh lived almost two hourse away, so she wasn't here for a flying visit.

"You can have a quick look around the house while I put the kettle on. We'll sit out on the terrace for coffee. It's lovely and warm there because of the old stone walls that enclose it."

After a quick tour of all of the rooms, Clodagh was back.

It was apparent to Ailish that she had something on her mind other than seeing the new house.

"What's up, Clo?"

"What? Oh, nothing, why do

you ask?"

"I haven't been your sister for all these years not to know when you are bottling something up. Do you want to share it now or will we have coffee and cakes first?"

"Clodagh?" Ailish ventured again when she saw her sister's face cloud over.

"Oh, Allie, I don't know what I am going to do. I promised to organise an excursion for my ladies' flower-arranging club and I totally forgot to book anything." Clodagh shook her head. "They all think they're going on a day trip to do something different and daring, and I haven't the heart to tell them that there is no trip planned at all!"

"Really, Clodagh, how could you forget?"

"I meant to write it down, but something came up and I forgot. Just yesterday, the chairperson phoned to confirm that she had twenty people booked in and that the bus was ordered. I didn't know what to say. So I just said, 'That's wonderful news.'

"I rang every hotel and event centre within a couple of hours, but no-one could take a group at such short notice. I couldn't sleep a wink last night worrying over it," she added gloomily.

"When are you supposed to be heading on the trip?" Ailish asked.

"Wednesday."

"This Wednesday? Clodagh, that's three days away!" Allison cried. "You'll have to phone the chairperson and tell her the truth."

"Allie, I can't, it's a fund-raiser for the local hospice. Nobody is ever going to trust me to organise anything again."

"And rightly so, I should think,"

Ailish replied.

Her sister looked miserable.

"Oh, come on. They will get over it," Ailish added.

This was so typical of Clodagh. Her heart was in the right place, but no sooner had she offered her help on one project than she had moved on to something else.

She was a total social butterfly but with a heart of gold.

Seeing her downcast face, Ailish softened. She was going to regret this, but she couldn't help herself.

"OK, I have an idea . . ." she heard herself say.

Clodagh's face lit up as she explained the plan to her.

"That is a fantastic idea! You're a lifesaver!" She clapped her hands in excitement. "I will organise the food and get extra tables and chairs if necessary."

Good humour restored, Clodagh left with her to-do list, and Ailish returned to the garden with renewed vigour.

● ● ● ●

Over the next couple of days, between working in the garden by day and poring over the kitchen table with paintbrush in hand by night, Ailish was just about ready.

On the Wednesday morning the bus pulled into the driveway.

The women descended, with Clodagh leading the pack.

Ailish noted with relief that they were all attired with sturdy footwear ready for their trek.

After a coffee on the terrace, they got their brief, collected a pack of treasure hunt clues, and set off towards the orchard.

"Not you, Clodagh," Ailish said firmly as she saw her sister reach for one of the packs. "It's the kitchen for you, my girl."

Clodagh laughed.

"Oh, yes. I nearly forgot that I'm supposed to be helping."

"Not helping, Clodagh. You're actually organising this event, remember?"

"Ailish, I owe you a big thanks for this." she said as she looked through a pack. "These really are brilliant. I think you could set up a new business if you wanted."

"The only business I'm interested in these days is getting my garden sorted. I'm only doing this as a favour for you, Clodagh.

"Now, we have twenty meals to prepare here, and you are in charge of everything foodwise."

"Let's have a coffee first," Clodagh replied. "We have loads of time before lunch. They will be ages solving all those clues and taking photos of each.

"You really are a clever thing." She laughed as she looked at the hand-painted illustrations that Ailish had included as part of the botanical treasure hunt.

"A vulpine creature wearing colourful mittens. Would that be a foxglove?" She laughed. "I'm better at this gardening lark than you give me credit for."

By the time the first of the ladies were back with all the clues completed, Ailish and Clodagh had lunch set up on the terrace.

The group were delighted with the gardens and with the treasure hunt.

They declared it the best fun they had had in ages.

The prizes were colourful plants Clodagh had managed to convince the local garden centre to donate.

Clutching these, they finally made their way towards the waiting bus in the late afternoon.

The chairperson thanked Ailish profusely for her hospitality and declared Clodagh the best event organiser ever.

Clodagh had the good grace to blush.

Finally, they were gone.

Ailish returned to the house, donned her gardening gear, and delved back into the garden.

She had only one day left before Hugo returned.

• • • •

The following evening, Ailish heard a familiar voice calling into the garden.

"I'm back! What a time I've had – I'm absolutely wrecked," Hugo announced, flinging himself into his favourite chair on the terrace.

"Fancy stopping for a nice cup of tea? I could really use one. I must say you have made some great progress in the garden.

"I really envy you all the free time you have at your disposal to indulge your true passion. Not a soul to interrupt your days.

"Hey why don't we eat out tonight, Allie?" he suggested. "We could try the new Italian restaurant in the village. My treat for abandoning you here on your own all week."

Ailish opened her mouth to correct him and then shook her head.

She chuckled.

"Yes, Hugo, that would be lovely. I could use a break from the garden."

Perhaps she would bring him up to date later on her "quiet" week over some nice Italian wine. ■

WATERFORD, COUNTY WATERFORD

WATERFORD, a historical city founded by Vikings in 914 AD, sits on the coast of south-eastern Ireland. The city's rich heritage is evident in its well-preserved medieval core, with landmarks like Reginald's Tower and the Viking Triangle.

Visitors can explore the city's museums, including the Medieval Museum, the Irish Museum of Time and the Bishop's Palace.

The House of Waterford Crystal showcases the renowned craftsmanship of Irish crystal. Visitors are welcome to enjoy tours at the factory.

The city was also once a hub for the wine trade, being a bustling port with thriving connections to Britain and the European mainland. Artefacts from this aspect of Waterford's history can be seen in the Medieval Museum.

Lost In A Maze

BY BECCA ROBIN

THE girls were so excited and chattering wildly in the back of the car. Lots of their friends had visited the sunflower maze at Goodbrooks Farm.

Now it was Faith and Lily's turn and, fortunately, Greg was home for the weekend so both he and Katie could take them.

"We're going to see the some flowers maze!" four-year-old Lily chanted.

"It's a sunflower maze, I keep telling you." Six-year-old Faith proceeded to try to give her sister an elocution lesson, but to no avail.

"Say 'sunflowers'."

"Some flowers!" Lily cried.

"Mummy, she's doing it on purpose!" But Faith couldn't help laughing along with everyone else.

"Pia said they're so tall, it's like being a little mouse." Lily wrinkled her nose and squeaked.

"Rowan in our class said he was lost for hours and hours until he found the middle," Faith added, not to be outdone.

"Well, I've packed our picnic rucksack, so when we do find the middle, we'll celebrate with something nice to eat." Katie turned and beamed at them. "Isn't it wonderful Daddy could come with us today?"

"Yay!" they both cheered.

"I wouldn't have missed it for the world."

Greg caught sight of the girls' contented smiles in the rear-view mirror.

He was so pleased he'd managed to do some juggling so his deputy could present his report at the meeting that day.

For once he didn't have to be there.

A few months ago Greg had been promoted, but the increase in pay and status had come at a cost.

These days he was away from home a lot, including more weekends than he'd been expecting.

Although the girls were young, they were both at school and growing fast.

Recently he'd missed important milestones like sports days and parents' evenings, and although she didn't grumble, it seemed unfair for Katie to cover it all by herself.

And it wasn't the same, wishing the girls goodnight via a video-call from a hotel bedroom a

Illustration: Ruth Blair.

hundred miles away.

There was a possible solution to the problem.

An interesting position had come up at a company closer to home, but it meant less money and status.

Katie was all in favour of it, but Greg wasn't sure. He could imagine what his colleagues would say. They'd think it such a backward step.

It was still early when they pulled into the car park.

Goodbrooks was a working farm that also provided visitor attractions, and the sunflower maze stood in one of the fields.

Greg had seen some drone footage online that showed intricately designed pathways winding between tall sunflowers in full, spectacular bloom.

There were supposed to be surprises at the dead ends and a picnic area in the middle.

They couldn't have chosen a better day: sunny with the sky a clear, cloudless blue.

When the girls got out of the car, Katie slathered them in extra suncream and they donned colourful hats and sunglasses.

Greg's heart melted at the sight of the girls heading off up the path in their jaunty holiday shorts and stripy T-shirts, wearing little rucksacks that contained water bottles and their favourite dolls.

Greg went to pay the girl sitting inside the wooden cabin in the car park.

Their family ticket covered not just the maze, but a visit to the cutting patch, where you could cut your own bunch of sunflowers to take home.

The maze wasn't far from the car park and, hearing the girls' shrieks of delight, Greg ran to catch them up.

A huge wall of sunflowers stood ahead with a sign saying *This Way* next to the entrance.

The flowers weren't just tall. Their leaves and stalks provided a dense cover that was impossible to see through.

"Let's go in!" Lily cried.

"All right, but we've all got to promise to stick together," Katie replied.

"We promise." Faith drew a speedy criss-cross on her chest. "Now let's go."

With terrible timing, Greg's phone rang.

Why on earth hadn't he switched it off, or at least set it to silent?

He could see the call was from Vanessa, his deputy.

"It's work." He sighed, and Katie groaned. "I'm sorry but I'd better answer it. You three go ahead."

It didn't seem fair to make the girls wait, and surely whatever the call was about, it wouldn't take long, and then he'd be able to catch them up.

Unfortunately the problem wasn't so straightforward.

Some figures had gone missing ahead of the meeting.

Luckily, Greg located the missing information in an electronic file he could access on his phone, then he rang Vanessa back.

It was a good 10 minutes before the problem was sorted and he could step into the maze.

Greg walked ahead 10 yards or so to where the path divided.

The sunflowers were so tall, it made you feel you'd shrunk like some fairytale character.

No wonder Lily's friend had felt like a mouse.

All at once, he heard an unmistakeable giggle a little way off.

It had to be Faith.

Greg stopped himself from calling out because that felt like cheating, and for the same reason he decided not to ring Katie on his mobile phone, which was now in his back pocket, set to vibrate.

He thought he could gauge which direction the giggle had come from, so he turned right at the fork in the path and carried on walking until he came to another junction.

This time he turned left.

Above his head, the golden sunflowers turned their stately faces towards their namesake on high.

Even though he hadn't gone far, Greg doubted he could have found his way back to the entrance.

He was already lost.

At least the morning sun was still in the eastern part of the sky, and he could use it to do a certain amount of navigating, perhaps.

After a few more twists and turns, he met a father and son coming the other way.

The little boy was about Lily's

112

age and was staring all around in wonder.

The path was only three feet wide, if you took into account the big leaves sticking out, and Greg flattened himself to one side to let them pass.

"Watch where you're going, Jamie," the father said, and he and Greg exchanged a smile.

Of course, it would be perfectly possible to push your way through a wall of plants, but that most definitely would have been cheating.

Even so, Greg almost felt like doing so when he heard Katie's voice a few feet away on the other side of the wall.

This time, he did call out.

"I'm here! Just trying to get to you."

"It's Daddy!" he heard Lily cry.

"I left something for you in the dead end," Faith yelled.

"Stay there, I'm coming. I'm only round the corner," Greg called back.

He sped up, but when he rounded the corner, he came up against another wall.

He could only turn right and carry straight on, before being forced into another right turn.

The maze certainly had been laid out in a fiendishly clever way.

Katie and the girls' voices were becoming more distant.

"Sorry, I'm heading further away from you!" he called.

"No, Daddy!" two little voices wailed.

"Don't worry," he called. "You carry on and I'll meet you in the middle."

The phone in his back pocket vibrated and he pulled it out.

Katie had taken a selfie with the girls.

They all looked adorably happy and excited, and the message accompanying the photo read, *Meet you in the middle for the picnic.*

Wasn't there some rule that if you kept turning in the same direction you would eventually end up in the middle of a maze?

It seemed worth a try, so Greg decided that whenever presented with a choice, he'd turn left.

The dark, leafy walls were becoming annoyingly monotonous, but only because he was so desperate to catch up with his family.

At one point he spotted a little girl who from a distance looked just like Faith.

But when he caught her up, he discovered the child was just wearing a similar red-and-white T-shirt and dawdling behind her own family.

He reached one of the dead ends and the surprise that awaited was a tree stump with a small fairy door attached to its side.

Although there was no-one around, Greg felt a little silly, crouching to open the door.

Inside was a beautiful hand-carved model of a fairy that would have delighted the girls, if they'd seen it.

As he was straightening up, Greg noticed something else: a piece of paper on the ground weighed down by a stone.

He unfolded the paper and read the message.

Daddy, don't be long! We want you with us! Love Faith, Lily and Mummy.

He kissed the paper, folded it

and put it in his breast pocket, next to his heart.

He wanted to be with them, too.

Wasn't this a similar feeling to one he'd been getting a lot lately on long car journeys and in anonymous hotel rooms?

He loved Katie and the girls so much, he longed to spend more time with them.

Greg carried on, sticking to his "turn left" rule.

There were more dead ends and more fairy doors, which by this stage were failing to enchant him.

He received another message from Katie, saying:

We're here. Where are you?

It was accompanied by a photo of the girls sitting on a blanket from home, tucking into the picnic.

The maze had started filling up with more people, and it didn't seem possible that Greg would hear Katie or the girls' voices now, amid the general hubbub.

Neither did he feel like calling out with so many others around.

The sunflowers didn't seem as charming any more. They looked like guards on duty, intent upon stopping him reaching his family.

He was almost on the point of giving up when he took a left turn and walked straight into the clearing in the middle of the maze.

Katie greeted him with a huge smile and the girls flung themselves at him as though he'd been missing for months.

"I'm so sorry." He dropped to his knees on the blanket.

"Don't worry. You've found us now." Katie poured him a coffee from the flask and passed it over.

"But I wanted to do this maze with you. That was the whole point."

"It's OK, Daddy. We can still find our way out together." Faith gave him a big kiss on the cheek.

"Have a blueberry." Lily popped one into his mouth.

Greg wrapped his arms around the two girls and hugged them, relieved his absence hadn't upset them too much.

Katie passed him a slice of homemade banana loaf and he leaned across and kissed her.

While the girls went off to explore the edges of the clearing, Greg turned to Katie.

"I'm tired of missing all the good stuff where my family's concerned," he said.

"Are you still thinking about that other job?"

Seeing him nod, Katie's smile widened.

"We did the sums," she reminded him. "The pay cut's doable if we tighten our belts. It would be wonderful to see more of you."

Greg wasn't just thinking about it: he'd reached his decision.

Later that evening, once the girls were in bed, he'd begin the application progress.

Once the remnants of the picnic were packed away, the four of them ventured back into the maze, ready for the fun of finding their way out.

Katie slipped her hand into his while Faith and Lily skipped ahead.

They were keen to get to the cutting patch to choose some sunflowers to take home.

This was the kind of day the girls would always remember, and Greg wouldn't have missed it for the world. ■

BALTO THE DOG

I**N** 1925, a diphtheria outbreak threatened the lives of thousands in Nome, Alaska. With traditional travel routes impassable, a daring plan was hatched: a dog-sled relay to transport life-saving serum from Anchorage.

Led by experienced mushers like Leonhard Seppala and his lead dog Togo, and Gunnar Kaasen and his young sled dog Balto, the teams braved harsh winter conditions, covering hundreds of miles.

Balto, despite his youth, led the final leg of the journey, delivering the serum to Nome in record time.

This heroic feat became known as the Great Race of Mercy, and Balto, the symbol of courage and perseverance, captured the hearts of the nation.

Image: Wikimedia Commons.

Between The Lines

BY H. JOHNSON-MACK

DEAREST Jane, I am writing to you from Bradings, where we have arrived safely, if rather chilled with all this rain!

It is lovely to be back here, though Cousin Celia's up to mischief again, determined to marry me off to whomever might take a fancy to me whilst I'm here.

But she does it so merrily, I still adore her!

Besides, as Mama's frustrations over my disappointing London season are well known, she and Aunt Mariah want to help by finding me a suitable husband.

Today, Celia took me to their modiste, De La Fleur. She's insisted on a new gown for me as an early birthday gift, and I cannot help being excited.

On the way home, we met Harry Dryden and the eldest Peveril – remember the Peverils from Wisden Grange?

It was quickly apparent that here were two of these eligible bachelors Celia is obsessed with, for herself as well as me.

"Why, Mr Peveril, I scarcely recognised you!" I blurted out, for Gilbert is now so tall and solid, his face so grave.

"What about me?" Harry asked.

I laughed.

"You may have fought a war, sir, but there's still that boyish mischief in your eyes I remember from childhood."

He seemed pleased by that and walked with me upon his arm all the way back to Bradings.

"Isn't Harry a dream?" Celia demanded when we were alone. "If he wasn't a younger son, I'd badger Mama to let him pay his addresses to me, but you know what she's like about position."

"What of his companion?" I asked.

"Oh, Gilbert's a dear, if so staid now. He had a hard war, Harry says, and was relieved to sell out early to take over his father's estate.

"I like his sister Eliza – remember her?" Celia went on. "You'll meet her tonight at dinner."

And so I did.

Eliza Peveril is taller than even you, Jane, and as bright as her brother is brooding.

I warmed to her immediately.

"I hope you like dancing," she said, sitting beside me, "for you must come to our traditional summer ball; the more,

Illustration by Shutterstock.

Set in
1815

the merrier."

Her brother approached the sofa.

"Let Miss Rawle alone, Eliza. She may not care for such things."

"On the contrary," I corrected him. "I adore dancing, or anything that brings a community together, particularly in the celebration of summer romance."

Eliza laughed.

"Look out, dear brother. Cupid's sharpening his arrows. Take care you are not hit by mistake."

Mr Peveril's sleek brows drew together.

"There's little chance of that."

His austere assurance made me mischievously quote from Shakespeare: "Love looks not with the eyes but with the mind."

After our meal, we repaired to the drawing-room and a merry fire for games.

It was great fun; I won at Speculation then promptly lost the pot!

Celia is a wonder at the game. She's so quick and seems to read everyone's minds.

"You and Harry made a good match," she observed as she brushed my hair for bed. "I'm almost jealous."

"He's as fast as you," I replied, "and funny, too. Does he ever take anything seriously?"

"It's his way of dealing with the horrors of Waterloo," Celia said, ➤

her eyes clouding. "A much nicer method than Gilbert's gravity, don't you think?"

I've been pondering this as I finish your letter and cannot decide.

To me, the fact that either man must find ways to deal with such demons is awful.

I must not end on a sad note, though, so will say we're visiting the old Maxstoke Priory tomorrow, which is supposedly lovely and worth sketching.

Hope all is well at home.

Yours affectionately, Emily.

• • • •

Dear Jane, it was wonderful to hear from you. I'm glad your cold has cleared up.

The priory ruins were indeed charming, with romantic crumbling tower and gothic window arches.

Bradings stables provided me with a sweet mare named Doe.

Harry Dryden rode between us, keeping us entertained with tales of hunts and horses.

At sight of Maxstoke's beauty, I disappeared with my sketchbook, where I lost myself until disturbed by a voice at my shoulder.

"Drawing, Miss Rawle? Is that not a little dull?"

I looked up at Gilbert Peveril.

"You have a misguided opinion of me, sir. I love to sketch and read, as much as I love to ride and dance."

He bowed.

"Perhaps we are both guilty of misjudgement. I, too, like to dance."

"Indeed? How daring of you!"

He was startled into a laugh.

"You claimed me changed, madam. I must be, if you cannot believe me capable of enjoying such things."

"Well," I said, closing my sketchbook, "you've certainly lost your smile somewhere in your travels."

I then went in search of Celia, glad to be in sight of her gaiety.

Something about Gilbert Peveril unsettled me.

Eliza joined us to discuss their forthcoming ball.

It sounds such fun, for in this recent inclement weather the whole community seems keen to celebrate something!

I thought of the fabled Cupid, flitting from place to place, seeking folk who could benefit from finding love.

Would he consider me a candidate, or anyone else in our party?

Celia or Harry seemed like the perfect choice.

There was an incident on the way home.

Doe took exception to a squirrel and shied so suddenly that I was almost unseated.

Luckily, Mr Peveril was quick to catch her bridle, his steadying motion enough to keep me upright and save my blushes.

I would have been more grateful, only he frowned so heavily that I kept my thanks to a minimum.

My birthday gift has just been delivered and it's divine!

White muslin with fern-embroidered hem and sleeves. I will save it for the ball.

Yours affectionately, Emily.

• • • •

Darling Jane, I write this at a sinfully late hour, but sleep eludes me. What a night it has been! Celia and I were like schoolgirls, ridiculously excited about the Peverils' ball.

But as she pointed out, we'd not been to a dance since Christmas.

Though she will always outshine me, my new dress and the way her maid fashioned my hair did give me some confidence in my appearance – a nice change!

Butterflies flitted in my stomach when we stepped into Peveril Hall's long ballroom bedecked in buttercup-and-green garlands and a hundred glittering candles.

Then came the biggest surprise of the night.

"May I have this dance?" Gilbert Peveril had threaded through the energetic dancers to me and extended his hand.

"Why, sir, I never thought to see you embracing such frolics!" I said to hide a blush. "Or are you here to support Eliza?"

"Not entirely for her," he said bluntly. "Not since you came."

For once I had naught to say.

I wasn't as surprised as I might have been when he turned out to be a wonderful dancer.

It stayed in my mind through my other partners, despite Harry Dryden's whirling and banter.

"What is it, love?" Celia asked in between tunes. "You look distracted."

"Have you ever had your first impressions overthrown? It's quite a dizzying experience."

"Find your feet," she said eagerly, "and tell me more."

But I couldn't form the words, so merely laughed and pushed her into Harry's waiting arms, which she was more than happy with.

I am sure that, younger son or no, Celia will persuade Aunt Mariah to accept her becoming Mrs Dryden before year's end!

And do I begrudge her Harry's charm? Of course not. My heart has found its own home in a most unlikely but wonderful place.

I had to wait some time, though, before he approached.

"At the risk of another misjudgement, Miss Rawle, I believe you are not too tired or unwilling to get some air with me?"

In answer, I held out my arm, which fitted in the crook of his.

We stood on the balcony as if we'd naught more on our minds than the fine night.

Then Gilbert finally spoke.

"You said I had lost my smile. I want to find it again, and I believe you could help me do so.

"I am not adept at pretty speeches, but if you'd marry me, Emily, I would do my best to improve."

"You're already better than you think," I replied, "and my answer is yes."

Then I touched my fingertip to his mouth.

"Oh, look, there's a piece of that missing smile already . . ."

You will meet Gilbert soon, my Jane, as we are both anxious to formalise things with our families, so I am coming home early.

Celia and Aunt Mariah are so excited by the match that they are practically packing my bags!

Who would have guessed that Cupid's mistake in striking Gilbert with a wayward arrow would end so romantically?

Until I see you, then, I am now his affectionately, Emily. ◼

Illustration: Shutterstock.

The Morning Post

Remember the regular morning post,
Read eagerly over tea and toast?
Gossip, secrets, plus all the news,
Invites, jokes and the latest views.

There's the sound of the letter-box clatter;
Penfriend stories full of chatter.
Greeting cards brought us cheer,
Caring thoughts throughout the year

Appointments were made,
Best plans laid,
New job offer, official on paper,
Love notes, too, all saved for later.

Now technology make messages instant;
The mail service is almost redundant.
Yet I still yearn for a nice long letter –
That personal touch was so much better!

BY S.BEE

Time Flies

BY BECCA ROBIN

"**G**RANNY!**" Two little voices rang out and footsteps hastened along the paths between the flower-beds.

"Well, what a treat," Penny said, rising from her kneeler to embrace Tammy and Casey. "I didn't expect to see you this afternoon.

"I thought you'd be getting ready for your friend's birthday party."

"We went to buy her present." Penny's daughter Gemma, who was carrying the shopping, caught up with them. "We're just calling by on our way home."

Penny was a volunteer in the physic garden that was a popular destination for day-trippers and townsfolk alike.

With its high stone walls and beds of fragrant medicinal plants, it was a little oasis of calm just off the bustling high street.

Resurrected in the 1990s, it stood on the ancient garden's original site, in the grounds of a long-demolished manor house.

It was free to enter.

"You're not here on your own, ❯

are you?" Gemma looked around and frowned.

"Oh, no. There's someone else here. I expect he popped out for a minute."

Although Penny smiled, she felt uncomfortable.

Every time her daughter appeared these days, Neil would disappear.

Of course she knew why, and he never made a big thing of it.

"What are you doing, Granny?" Tammy asked.

"Just tidying up this straggly chamomile before it takes over."

It was late summer and many of the plants were overblown.

Although the pot marigolds were still a golden riot, the ground was strewn with spent blooms.

Yet every time of year had its own charms.

Penny loved the rich haze of the purples and dark pinks that took over from mid-August, courtesy of the painted sage and echinacea.

Bees were in abundance, particularly in the lavender border.

The garden was laid out so the beds related to different parts of the body, containing plants that had treated ailments in the days before modern medicine.

Many plants appeared in more than one bed.

"Can I pick a flower?" Casey pointed at a nasturtium and Penny nodded.

The girls knew not to touch any plants without asking, as there were some poisonous specimens.

"What was chamomile used for?" Tammy asked.

"All sorts. Mainly tummy problems," Penny explained. "But you'll find it in the beds relating to the eyes, the liver and kidneys, infections . . ."

"There's the other volunteer." Gemma waved and Penny turned.

Neil had just entered at the other end of the garden.

After a brief wave, he began tidying a patch of unruly hollyhocks, the pods of which would dry out before the seeds were harvested.

"It's that man who lives down the road from us," Gemma remarked. "Mr Blake, isn't it? I've seen him here a few times."

"Oh, Neil's volunteered here for years." Penny tried keeping her voice light. "He showed me the ropes when I arrived."

This barely registered with Gemma.

She kissed her mother's cheek.

"Well, sorry we can't stop."

The girls were performing their little ritual before leaving: running round the plinth that stood in the middle of the garden.

"Granny, how does this thing work? I've forgotten." Tammy rested her chin on the metal plate atop the plinth.

Penny and Gemma went over.

"In the days before clocks, they used a sundial to tell the time," Penny said. "There should be a triangular thing called a gnomon on top, but according to people who've worked here a long time, it's been missing for ages.

She avoided saying Neil's name again.

"When the sun shines, the gnomon casts a shadow on the dial telling you what time it is."

"A gnome on top!" Casey shrieked, delightedly.

"Gnom-on. It's one word," her

elder sister corrected her. "And what does this mean, Granny?"

Her finger stroked the Latin engraved upon the metal in curly, copperplate script.

"Tempus," Penny said. "It means 'time'."

"Time you found the gnomon." Casey hooted with laughter and they all joined in.

After they'd gone, Penny noticed Neil sitting under the shelter at one end of the garden, pouring tea from his tartan flask.

She approached and sat beside him.

"You don't have to keep doing that," she said.

"Doing what?"

"Vanishing whenever my daughter's around."

Neil took a swig of tea.

He passed her the cup and she took a sip, knowing he wouldn't have indulged in this small but intimate gesture had Gemma been present.

"I feel awkward, pretending there's nothing going on between us," he admitted.

"It didn't seem to matter to begin with," he added, "but as time's gone by and I've fallen more in love with you, it feels wrong to pretend in front of your daughter."

Penny took a deep breath.

Her heart was too full to look at him, but she placed her hand lightly on top of where his rested on the bench.

"I'll tell her soon – when the time's right."

"It almost feels like you're ashamed of me." He offset this with a chuckle.

"Oh, don't say that. You know it's not true."

She removed her hand.

She couldn't tell him not to be silly when she sympathised with his point of view.

But what could she do or say about a situation that had been giving her sleepless nights?

She was a widow of five years and he a widower of seven.

Neil had already informed his son Alex about their relationship.

Alex was coming home from Canada at Christmas and apparently couldn't wait to meet Penny.

Why was it so difficult for Penny to tell her own family?

"Gemma idolised her dad," she explained. "They had such a special bond."

"Gemma's an adult." Neil turned to face her. "She must realise you could meet someone else.

"Of course she loved her dad, but she loves you, too. She'd want you to be happy, surely?"

"I fully intend telling her." Penny still couldn't look at him. "Like I said, I'm just waiting for the right time."

"And when will that be?"

They returned to their respective tasks, but the sky had clouded over and there was a chill in the air.

In the beginning, the secrecy had only added to the excitement of their new romance.

Stolen kisses in the greenhouse and barely perceptible looks and smiles when they passed one another in public had only added to the frisson.

But Neil was right – their relationship had moved up a level.

He'd been patient for weeks

when, in his words, all he'd wanted to do was sing of his love from the rooftops.

So what was Penny afraid of? Upsetting her only child? That an argument might sour her and Neil's relationship; risked bursting their love bubble?

It didn't help that Neil and Gemma lived in the same street.

Penny had never visited his house and was reluctant to have him at hers, lest her daughter should call unexpectedly.

Sometimes they'd go to a café and hold hands under the table.

But even then Neil must have guessed why she never wanted to sit in the window.

No wonder he was fed up.

He'd asked a reasonable question: when could she foresee the right time to tell Gemma?

Unfortunately she didn't know the answer.

"I'm sorry." She heard Neil's voice and turned to find him smiling in a sad way. "I don't want to put you under pressure."

"No, I'm sorry." She straightened up. "I don't know why I'm so scared."

"It's a big change," he replied. "And it might take Gemma a while to adjust to the idea. I understand why it's scary."

There was no-one around, so they embraced.

A couple of days later, Gemma and the girls appeared mid-morning.

The girls had just come from their swimming class and were in high spirits.

They played hide and seek, with Tammy being the first to stand beside the sundial, cover her eyes and count to a hundred, while Casey went to hide behind a big patch of comfrey.

Penny sat with Gemma in the shelter.

Her stomach clenched when Neil put down his wheelbarrow and approached.

"Lovely day, isn't it?" Neil pulled off his gloves and extended his hand. "I'm Neil. I don't think we've met."

"I'm Gemma, Penny's daughter." She shook his hand. "Mum was saying you've volunteered here for years."

"For my sins." Neil chuckled. "I love it. It's a special place; a place where time stands still."

"Perhaps if you found the missing part of the sundial . . ." Gemma began.

"Yes, it's a real puzzle."

He told the story of how, years before, a volunteer had taken the sundial apart to clean it, only to find the gnomon he'd left on the ground had vanished.

They'd expected it to turn up, but it hadn't, and now everyone assumed it was gone for good.

Penny was only half listening.

Wasn't Neil being far too attentive for someone who'd just stopped for a casual chat?

She was relieved when he left.

"What a nice man, Mum," Gemma remarked. "He's ever so friendly, isn't he?"

"Hmm? Oh, yes."

Fortunately, Gemma changed the subject and soon she and the girls left for home, with Neil waving them off in a hearty fashion from where he was digging in the bed.

It had a little slate sign saying, *Ailments Of The Heart*.

Penny walked over to him.

"Didn't overdo it, did I?" he asked.

"Maybe a little," she replied.

Neil sighed.

"Sorry, Penny. You tell me off when I avoid her and when I make an effort, it's too much."

"I didn't mean to upset you."

He left his spade in the earth, walked over, removed his gloves and took her hands in his.

"It's impossible to act naturally around you. I love you too much."

"I'm sorry, Neil. I'm just waiting for the right time to tell her."

His incredulous look said it all.

The situation was clearly stressing Neil out, so it wasn't a surprise when he ducked out of his next shift at the physic garden.

I know Gemma and the girls are coming for a picnic, he texted. *Concentrate on them and have a lovely time. I'll ring you later.*

She knew he wasn't being deliberately awkward, and she felt terrible.

Neil didn't know where to put himself in this equation, and now it was driving him away from the place he'd always loved.

Well, at least she could help with the task he'd begun.

Fetching the tools from the shed, she began work, digging out a dead bush from the heart bed.

All at once her spade struck something hard, which made a ringing sound.

She uncovered the straight edge of a metallic object.

More digging released it and when she wiped away the dirt, she was stunned . . .

• • • •

It was two o'clock and the girls had finished eating and were chasing each other around the beds when Neil arrived.

Penny could tell her recent text had hit home, since he approached their picnic blanket with visible trepidation.

She and Gemma rose to their feet.

"Mum's told me." Gemma smiled. "And I couldn't be happier."

Penny rushed into his arms and Gemma joined them in a group hug.

"I'm so glad," Neil said through tears of joy. "But I'm curious. What made it the right time to reveal all?"

"This," Penny said, leading him to the middle of the garden.

Her text message hadn't told him everything.

There was the gnomon, slotted back in place on top of the sundial, casting its shadow and marking the time of day.

It just required a small screw to secure it.

"I found it when I was digging in the heart bed," Penny said. "Do you remember the Latin word inscribed upon it? It's what made me brave enough to tell Gemma."

"I'm not sure I do," Neil admitted.

Penny pointed at the Latin on the side of the gnomon: the word *Fugit*, to partner *Tempus* on the metal plate of the sundial.

"Tempus Fugit," Penny said. "Time flies.

"I needed reminding of that. And I can't let it fly away without acknowledging I've met someone I care about deeply."

Then it felt so good, in full view of the world, to place her hand proudly in his. ∎

Believe In Yourself

"Believe you can and you're halfway there" –
Some words I read each day,
And when the path is rough ahead
They help me find the way.
Believe you can, believe you're strong,
You always will win through,
No matter what tomorrow brings
It's really up to you.
Believe you can discover joy
And share the love you find,
And every day in every way
You'll find new peace of mind!

Iris Hesselden

Illustration by Shutterstock.

THE LAB MOUSE

A **QUIRKY** statue in Novosibirsk, Russia, honors the humble lab mouse. Unveiled in 2013, it depicts a wise-looking, elderly mouse knitting a DNA strand. The statue sits outside the Institute of Cytology and Genetics, and is a testament to the role mice play in scientific research. From disease studies to medication development, these small creatures have greatly contributed to human health, even if not by choice.

The statue was made by sculptor Alexei Agrikolyansky.

Whilst we seek alternative and species-appropriate ways of testing these days, this monument serves as a reminder of the often-overlooked sacrifices made by these wee animals in the pursuit of human progress.

Image: Shutterstock.

Sowing The Seeds

BY TERESA ASHBY

'VE got a surprise for you!"
John called from the end of
the garden. "Close your eyes."
Nella knew he was up to
something when he'd bustled
down the garden earlier,
clutching a sharp knife.

She smiled. Whoever would
have thought she'd say John and
bustled in the same sentence?

This was the man who used to
spend every lunch hour at the
gym, and often every weekend,
too, yet he'd never looked in
better shape.

She shielded her eyes from the
low September sun and tried to
see what he was up to.

"Close your eyes, I said!" he
called out.

Two years ago she'd have told
him off for telling her what to do,
but now she laughed and cupped
her hands over her eyes.

Two years ago, they hadn't
exactly been on the brink of
divorce after only a year of
marriage, but things had been
pretty shaky for a while.

She knew what the surprise
was. She'd seen a flash of orange
a few moments ago and knew
he'd harvested one of his
pumpkins.

He was so proud of them, and

rightly so. They'd grown round
and fat over the summer.

Rather like herself, Nella
thought, as her hand fell to her
growing bump.

"No peeking," John said, and
she put her hand over her eyes
again.

Two years ago, they'd barely
been speaking, yet in the weeks
before that, as they decorated
and furnished their home, they'd
done nothing but laugh and chat
and sing along to the radio.

The trouble had started on the
day that John vanished in the
jungle that was their back garden.

Nella thought she'd lost him.

It was a feeling that didn't go
away even when he reappeared
15 minutes later, a mixture of
cobwebs and leaves in his hair
and stains all over his white
T-shirt.

Normally if he got into such a
state, he'd have rushed off to
have a shower.

He'd gone in as the man she
adored, but had emerged as
someone she didn't recognise.

"I was about to send in a search
party," Nella had told him. "Why
didn't you answer when I called
you? I thought you'd fallen down
a hole or been abducted by aliens

Illustration: Pat Gregory.

or something."

"I was in the shed," he replied.

"Shed? I didn't know there was a shed."

The house had stood empty for a long time when they first viewed it.

Nella had looked down from the back bedroom window at a tangle of vines and brambles joining one tree to another like a gigantic green spider's web.

"It's buried in the undergrowth," John told her, pulling a prickly twig from behind his ear and wincing slightly. "It's very well built, so we'll definitely keep it once we've uncovered it."

"Did you find anything else on your adventures?"

"I did." He grinned. "There are garden tools in the shed and they were put away clean. Whoever used to live here loved the garden.

"There are two garden chairs that are a bit cobwebby, but I can clean them up. Oh, and I found this."

He looked like a little boy digging for treasure as he delved into his pocket and pulled out a small tatty notebook.

"'Walter's Garden Notes'," he said, reading out the words written on the front. "It's crammed with information about what to plant and when.

➤

"Obviously tried and tested. I can't wait to get started on my vegetable patch."

"Your vegetable patch?" Nella asked, her tone sharpening. "I thought we'd planned a lawn and a flower border with a water feature and a fire pit."

Her visions of sitting out to enjoy the garden in summer wafted away like a dandelion clock on the breeze.

"That would be such a waste of the land," John explained. "Look. He writes here about how he always had enough produce for the house and some to give away."

"But we can buy –"

John tutted.

"Did you just tut?" Nella laughed incredulously. "Did you really tut at me?"

They'd never had a serious argument before, but one was developing like a gathering storm.

All the while, John kept flapping that silly little book about as if it was the fount of all knowledge.

They still weren't speaking when they went to bed that night.

Nella was angry. Everything else they'd done since they'd been together had been a team effort.

Since moving into the cottage, they'd chosen paint and picked carpets together.

It had all been part of the fun of setting up home, but somehow John had decided the garden would be his domain.

He'd be demanding she fetched him his pipe and slippers next.

Except he didn't smoke a pipe and he always went barefoot around the house.

In the morning, they ate breakfast in silence.

"I know you don't want to talk about it, Nella, but that notebook is something special."

"Is it really?" she asked, as if she couldn't be less interested.

"It dates back further than the previous owners. It's almost a historical document."

She didn't want to admit she was curious.

John fished it out of his pocket.

It really was tiny, as small as a pocket diary, but quite thick with extra pieces of paper folded and hidden inside.

He opened it and some of the papers fluttered to the floor, brown and crisp with age.

Walter Ward, 1899, it read.

"That can't be the date!" Nella exclaimed. "And if it is, shouldn't you be handling it wearing gloves?"

John took out a folded piece of paper and carefully opened it.

"It's a plan of the garden. It's all been so carefully done, but it's quite faded. This is where he planted everything from fruit trees to onions."

"Where are the flowers?" Nella asked.

John made a noise. It sounded like a snort.

"Flowers?"

"I thought we were going to have a traditional cottage garden with tall, spiky flowers and lavender and snapdragons."

He looked at her as if she were mad.

"Until I found this book I didn't even think we could grow our own food, but it's been done. Tried and tested," he repeated.

"Think of the money we'd save. If we grow fruit, we could make jam and crumbles."

"Couldn't we have a vegetable patch and a flower garden?" Nella asked plaintively.

"Sorry, love. The garden isn't big enough for both," John replied. "Perhaps we could get you a couple of planters to put next to the back door and you could grow some flowers."

Nella stared at John in disgust. What had happened to him?

It was as if he'd had a personality transplant and had turned into the sort of man who placates the little woman with a couple of pots!

"I'm going to work," she muttered, jumping to her feet and gathering her things. "Don't forget it's your turn to cook dinner tonight."

At the local newspaper office where she worked, Nella's friend and colleague, Denise, asked what was wrong.

"You look as if you've lost a doughnut and found a sprout," Denise said in her usual cheerful manner. "Come on. Spill."

"I've had an argument with John. Sort of."

"Hold the front page!" Denise exclaimed, spinning her chair around. "Married couple falls out!"

Nella felt hurt. Arguments might be part of life for some people, but she hated confrontation almost as much as she hated giving in.

"Don't laugh at me," she said, struggling to hold back tears.

Denise leaned on the desk, all the laughter gone from her eyes.

"Is it really that serious? It can't be. You've only been married five minutes and you've just finished doing up your dream cottage. You should be in clover."

"Huh! More likely up to our ears in brassicas," Nella replied. "He found this book and he's gone all weird."

Denise pulled a face.

"What sort of book?"

"A notebook. It belonged to a previous owner of the cottage."

"Oh, do tell. Is it a diary? A work of fiction?" she asked. "Perhaps we could run a story on it. It would be great to track down the writer's family."

"No, it wouldn't," Nella retorted.

She was about to explain to Denise why she was upset and thought she might sound silly.

"Forget it. I'm sure we'll be fine."

"Of course you will." Denise nodded. "You're the dream team, you and John."

That's what Nella had always thought.

Up until now they'd been on the same wavelength, but finding that notebook had sent him veering off in the opposite direction.

She decided to have a proper conversation with John that evening.

Surely they could reach a compromise that suited them both.

He was right – they didn't really have room for a separate vegetable patch if she wanted her cottage garden.

Perhaps she should tell him to grow his courgettes in planters.

She smiled at that thought.

"That's more like it,"

Denise said.

When Nella got home, John was nowhere to be found and there was nothing cooking in their kitchen.

Perhaps he'd decided to get a takeaway.

Then she heard the sound of machinery and saw him in the garden, pushing a rotovator through the undergrowth.

She hurried outside.

"I'm home," she said, tapping him on the shoulder.

John jumped in the air and spun round.

He was wearing goggles and ear protectors.

"You made me jump! Is it that time already?" he asked once the rotovator was switched off. "I went to the hire shop and ordered this at lunchtime. I got to work as soon as I got home."

"What about the gym?"

"I cancelled my membership," he admitted. "If I'm going to get this garden sorted out, I'll have no time for all that."

"But you love the gym," Nella pointed out.

"A man can change, can't he?"

She was warmed by the grin she'd fallen in love with, but alarmed that someone could change quite so much.

"Sorry I'm late," she said. "I sent you a message."

"My phone's in my pocket. I wouldn't have heard it."

"So I'm guessing there's no dinner."

"Sorry, love. I lost track of time. Why don't you pop to the chip shop?" he suggested. "I'll have a battered sausage."

She could have been mean and got him a sausage and no chips,

but he looked worn out and there was no doubt he'd been working hard.

When she got back and they sat down to eat, she told him about her day at work.

"Sounds good," he replied. "Did I tell you that Mr Soames next door is going to give me some seeds and plants? Runner beans and the like?

"He says everything he grows in his garden was from cuttings or seeds from this one."

"Can't you talk about anything else?" Nella asked, picking up her plate. "I'm going to eat this in front of the telly. I'll leave you to think about your vegetables."

The annoying thing was, that was exactly what he did.

• • • •

At the weekend a skip was delivered, and John was still rotovating.

Nella decided to check out the attic.

They hadn't been up there yet, but she wanted to see if there was any useful storage space.

To her delight, the attic had been floored so would be an idea place for boxes.

She shone her torch round and saw something almost hidden beside the water tank.

Carefully she reached out, aware that there were probably big spiders living up there.

It was a notebook. Bigger than the one John had found, but not by much.

As she brushed away a layer of dust, Nella realised the book had been carefully covered in wallpaper.

She laughed and she was sure

John would laugh, too, when she told him.

From her bedroom window, she could see John still hard at work.

He was doing a great job clearing the garden, but she hated the thought of looking down on rows of carrots and cabbages when she'd been looking forward to hollyhocks and honeysuckle.

She opened the notebook.

Angela Blake, 1965, it read.

The pages were filled with neat writing and Nella felt like an intruder as she began to read.

If I don't write this down, I think I might kill him!

He's been driving me mad since he found that wretched notebook in the shed.

Now he wants to create the garden exactly as it was in Walter Ward's day, whoever he might have been!

Nella could tell how cross Angela must have been from how much her pen had dented the page.

Like Nella, she'd moved into the cottage after it had stood empty for a long time.

And like Nella, she'd looked forward to creating a cottage garden.

The more she read, the more she knew she couldn't mention the notebook to John.

Within the pages she found the solution to their problem.

"Thank you, Angela," she murmured.

Later, she'd pop the notebook back in the attic for when she and John eventually moved out.

It would be there for the next owners to find, but hopefully that wouldn't be for a very long time.

From now on, Nella decided not to moan about the vegetable patch.

Instead, she thought with a secretive smile, she'd make the best of it.

• • • •

The next spring, as John's vegetables began to grow, he noticed other things coming up all round the garden and rubbed his head.

"I'm not sure what this is," he said. "It doesn't look very carroty."

"That will be marigolds," Nella replied. "They're good to have in a vegetable garden.

"They keep certain pests away, and if you want to be organic, then that's good, isn't it?"

"I'll leave them in, then," he said.

And so flowers began to grow.

Sunflowers grew tall and strong, shading the pumpkin patch and attracting lots of bees.

In fact, all the flowers brought in ladybirds, hoverflies and other beneficial insects.

Not only that, it looked pretty, too, with everything mixed in together.

"I don't understand how they got here," John told her. "So many flowers, but they don't look out of place at all, do they?"

"Sometimes these things just happen. Nature lends a hand," Nella remarked vaguely.

"Yes, I think you're right." He grinned. "I wonder if the seeds were in the soil when I turned it over. We should let the flowers seed so they come up again next year."

He put his arm around her and pulled her close.

"I think we should have a seating area," he said. "Somewhere we can relax and enjoy our garden."

"That sounds wonderful."

And what was really wonderful was eating tomatoes and radishes fresh from the garden in their summer salads.

Their home-grown raspberries and strawberries were delicious, and there was something special about cooking dinner and asking John to pop out and dig up some potatoes and carrots.

That was last year. This year, the garden was even more their own.

Nella had a wisteria that would eventually grow around the kitchen door, and a lovely patio area with several planters brimming with colour.

So much for the two pots John had initially suggested, she thought with a wry smile.

John loved the flowers, too, and welcomed all the bees and butterflies that came to visit.

Nella had almost gone wrong, but Angela's little book had put her straight.

There didn't have to be any more arguments – just a realisation that they could have the best of both worlds.

Angela had sown seeds of her own amongst the vegetables and reported in her notebook that her husband was delighted with them.

Nella had done the same.

There were no regimented rows of anything, but the garden was a riot of shapes and colours.

•　•　•　•

"Open your eyes," John said now, and Nella took down her hands. "Voila!"

"Wow, John! That pumpkin is huge."

"Beautiful, isn't it?" He grinned.

"That will be because of the sunflowers casting the shade," Nella said with a smile.

She'd looked it up online and it was called companion planting.

"I'm sure you're right," he agreed. "But now the question is what are we going to do with this?"

"Pumpkin pies?" Nella suggested. "Pumpkin soup?"

"I would have saved it for Hallowe'en, but it was ready to be cut."

"We still can. It'll keep a while longer. When the time comes we'll make it into a lantern, put it by the front door so people will know we welcome trick or treaters."

"We might end up with a whole family of lanterns."

John laughed and Nella's hand fell to her bump again.

"Oh, I hope so," she said as John sat down beside her with a happy sigh. "Wouldn't that be just perfect?"

Perhaps most perfect of all was the play area John was already planning for the baby.

The garden bore no resemblance at all to the one charted in Walter's book, but it was all their own.

And it might not be very big, but it was beautiful.

She had a feeling that even Walter, with his meticulous plans, would approve, and she knew Angela would.

And just like the flowers and the vegetables, Nella and John would grow together, as good companions always do. ◼

KING PUCK

PUCK FAIR, Ireland's oldest festival, is a unique celebration. For three days, a wild mountain goat is crowned King Puck and placed on a high stand in the town of Killorglin. The goat, captured from the nearby Macgillycuddy's Reeks, is a symbol of fertility and is treated with reverence, but there's another story that explains its importance.

Oliver Cromwell was on his way to capture the town of Killorglin. His army frightened some wild goats and sent one fleeing into town. The citizens sensed something was up and scrambled to action, scuppering Cromwell's mission.

In recent years, concerns about animal welfare have led to changes in the tradition. The goat now spends less time on the stand and its overall treatment has improved.

Image: Shutterstock.

On The List

BY CHARMAINE FLETCHER

SOMETIMES I wish you would just kick the bucket, Jan."

Jan's pen hovered over her notepad, wondering if she'd heard Kit right.

"Don't tell me those commercials for over-fifties' life assurance have got to you," she replied. "Did you insure me and fancy running off to Rio with the proceeds?"

"No, love." He sighed, depositing a box of bric-a-brac on to the floor. "It's just that this is the last of Mum's stuff I've cleared out of our garage.

"I've been meaning to get rid of it for ages. Most of it is for the dump, but it's a shame.

"Lots of it has never been opened," he added sadly, nudging an unused box of Chanel No.5 scent, the Cellophane yellowing."

"Well, she did like saving things for best or putting them away for a rainy day."

"That's just it." Kit replied. "The waste aside, it seems that the time was never right for her. It's so sad."

"Maybe," Jan began, "she was simply one of those people who enjoyed knowing they had

something special tucked away without any need to actually use it. Like a dieter with a bar of chocolate in the fridge.

"They might never eat it, but it makes them feel secure, I suppose, knowing that it's there," she added. "I mean, look at my bucket list. I've had such fun adding things to that.

"Nothing fantastical, of course, but numerous other things I'd like to do one day when I've got the time." She smiled wistfully.

"That's what I mean about kicking the bucket – not dying, but just stop planning and start doing before it's too late," Kit explained.

"I do understand, but when?" she pointed out. "With my part-time job and your occasional book-keeping, how can we?

"Between work and hobbies, plus chores, there's not time to go swanning off on a whim."

"Listen to yourself, Jan," Kit replied. "The whole point of easing into retirement was to take on fewer responsibilities.

"As for the housework – well, the dust will still be here when we're gone."

Guiltily, Jan looked at the list she was adding to.

Illustration by Manon Gandiolle/Shutterstock.

This time it was macramé.

She'd tried it in the Seventies, but she'd never got the hang of it and hated being beaten.

As usual Kit had a point, but there was always so much to do . . .

Kit glanced down at Jan's growing bucket list.

"See – that's exactly my point!" he exclaimed. "Why not get on with it now?

"Here," he went on. "Let's forget about taking this lot to the dump and do something you've always wanted to instead."

"Like what?" she asked. "These things take planning. Besides, I'm not really dressed for anything."

"You look fine and so do I. Come on – let's not waste a minute more."

Kit glanced at Jan's list, noticing the subheading *Places To Go.*

"Caldwell Hall," Kit said enthusiastically. "The stately pile where they film that drama series you're always swooning over.

"It's not very far away, and it's a gorgeous morning, too."

He glanced at his watch.

"If we leave now there will be time for elevenses, a stroll in the gardens and a tour of the house.

"What do you say?"

"OK," Jan agreed finally.

"That's my girl!" Kit replied, grabbing his car keys and phone.

● ● ● ●

"There are a lot of cars here already," Jan said when they

arrived. "I hope it's not too busy.

"I hate it when places are full: a quick, stuffy tour then nowhere to sit in the restaurant.

"Still, that's what happens if you don't plan matters."

"Don't be so pessimistic. You've no evidence of that yet," Kit told her, raising his eyes heavenwards.

"No, but perhaps we should have waited and organised it better," Jan replied tersely, easing herself out of the car.

"Well, we're here now, so let's get our tickets and a programme. I hear they sell bedding plants and herbs, too – I'll be able to re-stock the greenhouse."

As they reached the ticket kiosk, apart from a few knots of people it was deserted.

"You see," Jan admonished. "I said we should have thought about it a bit more before just taking off like that –"

"Don't worry. I'll –" Kit placated, but before he could finish they were approached by a flustered-looking girl with a clipboard.

"You are the replacement background artists, aren't you?" she asked, seeing the bewilderment on their faces. "If not, I'm done for – this is the third time in a month they've gone AWOL.

"If it happens again, they'll sack me."

"We're just –" Jan began.

"Caldwell Hall is shut for the day so we can wrap up this season's filming of 'Passion At Pausley Place'," the girl continued. "Only we need the background artists for continuity in the ballroom scene."

"Well, we're –"

"Delighted to step in – we're a bit rusty on the old lines front but we'll work just fine with the right direction," Kit said quickly.

"Live a little," he whispered to Jan.

"Marvellous!" The girl beamed. "I'm Carrie, by the way, a production assistant.

"Follow me. We'll arrange some ID, then I'll get you both to wardrobe."

"Carpe diem," Kit told Jan quietly, "Besides, it's something to tell the grandchildren."

Once they were costumed and made up, Kit, Jan and the other background artists assembled outside the entrance to the hall.

"In this scene," the director was saying, "you are all guests arriving for the Pausley Place summer ball.

"It is the biggest event in the social calendar, so when I shout 'Action!', I want you all to sound politely excited."

"What's that when it's at home?" Jan said from the corner of her mouth.

"Just copy the others," Kit replied.

"Later in the scene . . ." The director went on scanning the crowd, ". . . Lady Marvel is swept up by Sir Simon De Vane and carried from the room and into his carriage.

"It is shocking, so when I say 'React!' I want gasps and lots of remarks.

"We'll shoot the arrivals first. Take your instructions from Tony over there." He nodded at a red-haired man. "And next time I see you, you'll be in the ballroom.

"There are chalk cross 'marks' as usual; don't move from them once in position. Remember this is a continuity shoot for the main players. Break a leg!"

"But it's broad daylight. Surely a ball would take place in the evening?" Jan hissed.

"Post production day for night." The woman next to her smiled. "It's amazing what they can do now."

"You learn something new every day," Kit said while they lined up, taking their places as instructed.

They entered and exited several times, once rehearsing and then until it was exactly right and everyone was in the correct place.

Next came the ballroom scene.

Jan was so thrilled to see her favourite actor and actress in their passionate clinch that she didn't have to feign excitement.

"React!" the director yelled.

"Well I never!" Jan said, her face to the camera.

"No, and you wouldn't have done, if I hadn't badgered you," Kit, standing opposite her, mouthed.

Suddenly, in a rustle of taffeta, Jan watched, amazed, as the hero gathered up the heroine from the clutches of her bullying husband as he strode through the ballroom and out to his carriage.

As instructed, everyone oozed shock and consternation, chattering in scandalised tones, until the director shouted, "Cut!"

Briefly the cast relaxed before the director yelled, "Right! Let's go again!"

As people took their places, Jan was amazed at the attention to detail for even the quickest scene screen-wise, and how many times things were repeated.

By six o'clock it had been a long day's filming, but everyone still had energy for the wrap-up party afterwards.

"I'll sort out your pay in a moment. It's only the casual rate, I'm afraid," Carrie said apologetically. "Then, once you've returned to wardrobe and make-up, the party's over there in that tent."

She pointed to a large marquee, lit up with brightly coloured bulbs.

"There are canapés, desserts, champagne, the usual," she added, waving her hands descriptively before heading towards the onsite office.

• • • •

"It's a shame there's no falling-over juice for me," Kit said regretfully as the champagne waiter passed, refilling Jan's glass in the process.

"Well, you are driving." Jan winked. "Besides, we've had such a wonderful day. Who needs alcohol really?"

Kit smiled down at her then frowned.

"What's that doing here?" he asked, nodding at her bucket list notebook.

"Look," she said, flipping through it. "I used the blank pages to get cast autographs."

"Don't you need it?"

"No, I know what I'll be doing in the future."

"How will you remember it all?" he asked.

"Because it starts tomorrow – from now on, no more waiting for me!"

"Now that's the sort of action I like to hear!" Kit grinned. PF

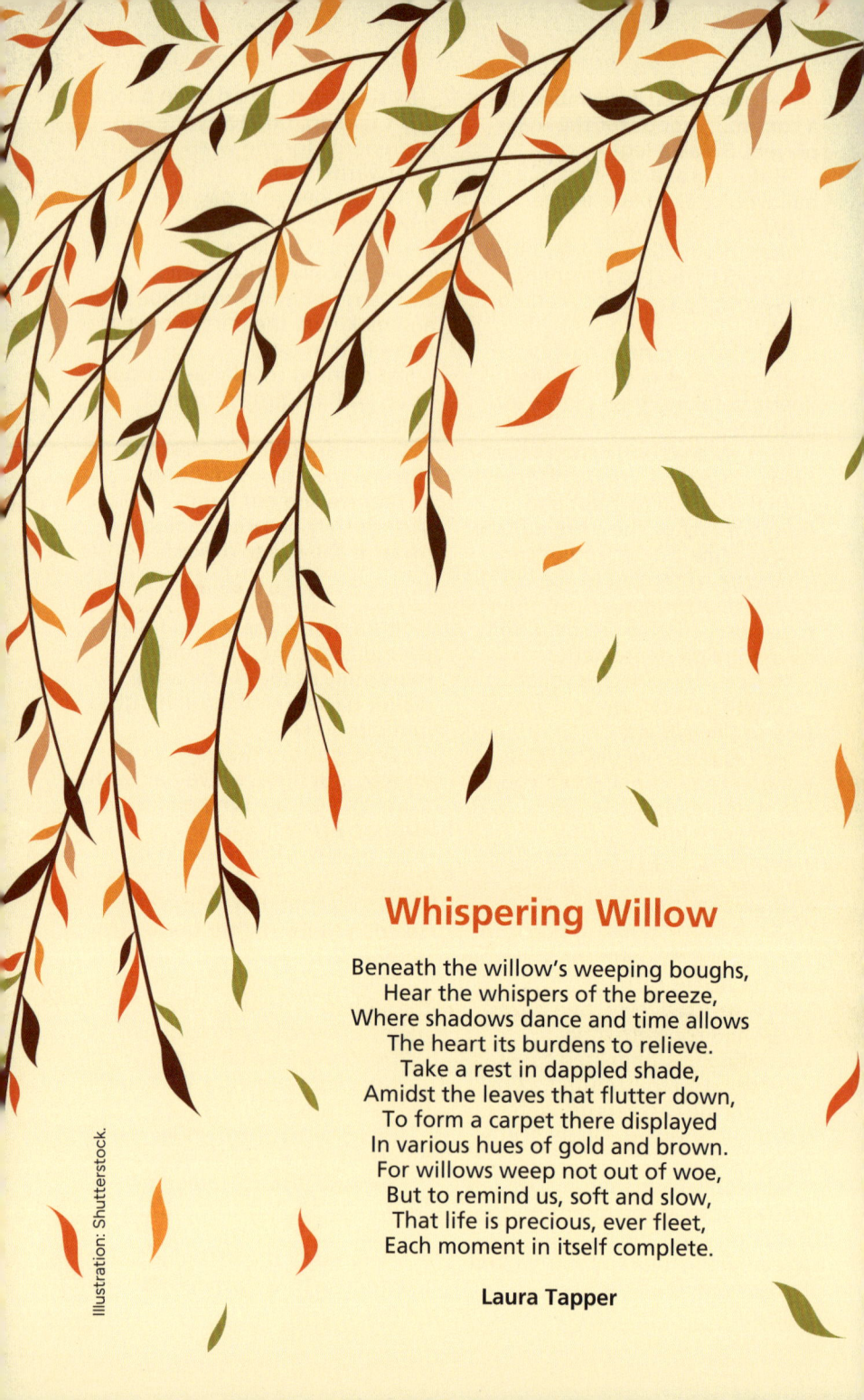

Illustration: Shutterstock.

Whispering Willow

Beneath the willow's weeping boughs,
Hear the whispers of the breeze,
Where shadows dance and time allows
The heart its burdens to relieve.
Take a rest in dappled shade,
Amidst the leaves that flutter down,
To form a carpet there displayed
In various hues of gold and brown.
For willows weep not out of woe,
But to remind us, soft and slow,
That life is precious, ever fleet,
Each moment in itself complete.

Laura Tapper

LYNMOUTH, DEVON

THE picturesque village of Lynmouth, nestled on the rugged North Devon coast, is a tranquil escape. Its charming streets, quaint cottages and stunning coastal scenery are a lovely combination.

The village's history is marked by both beauty and tragedy. The devastating 1952 flood had a lasting impact, but the strong community has rebuilt and thrived. The Memorial Hall marks this event and serves as a reminder of the area's resilience.

Lynmouth is connected to the nearby village of Lynton by a unique water-powered funicular railway, offering breathtaking views of the surrounding landscape.

The South West Coast Path passes through the area, providing opportunities for scenic walks and hikes.

Visitors can explore the Valley of Rocks, a dramatic landscape with towering cliffs and unique rock formations.

The area has inspired writers and poets, including Samuel Taylor Coleridge and William Wordsworth.

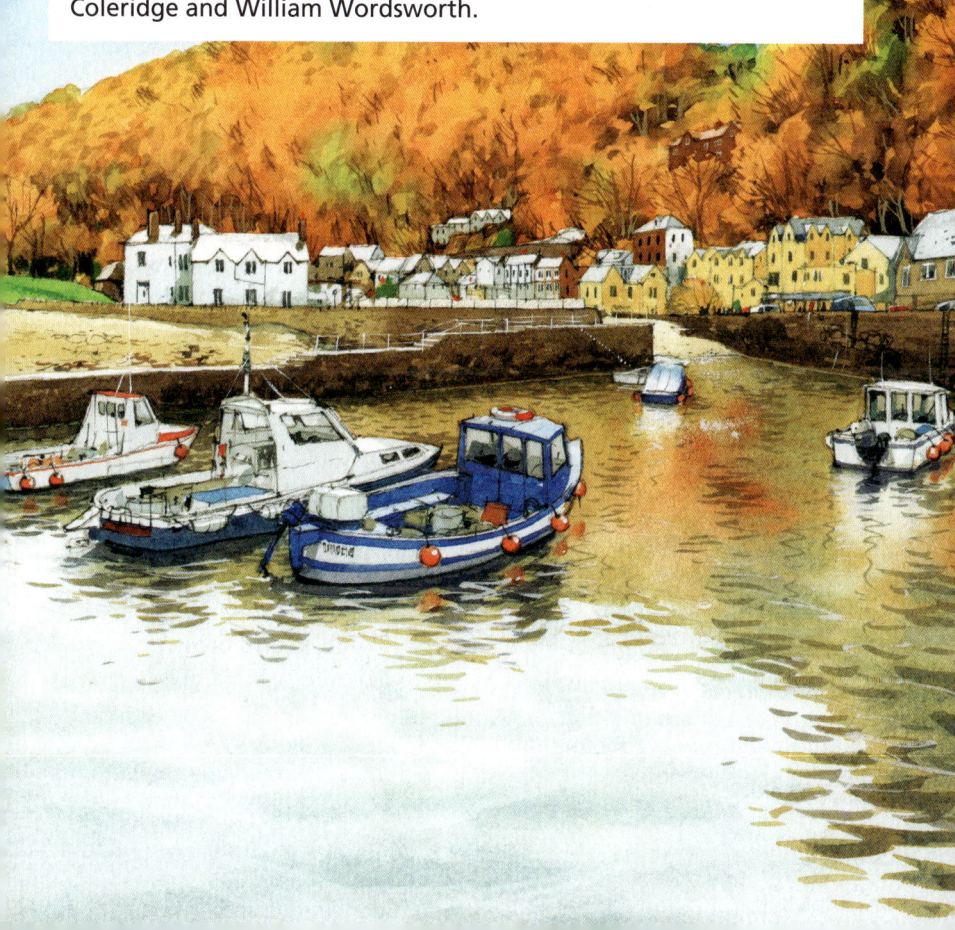

A Fresh Page

BY LYNNE HALLETT

HAILEY glanced up at the cuckoo clock on the wall opposite the counter and smiled. Just a minute till closing. It had been a strange old day – either extremely busy or deathly quiet – but owning a bookshop didn't always mean a steady stream of customers.

She moved from behind the counter just as the cuckoo popped out, but before she could change the sign to *Closed*, the door was flung wide open by a man who nearly fell into the shop.

"Thank heavens," he said, gasping for breath. "I thought you'd be shut."

"A few more seconds and I would have been."

"Sorry," he managed in between breaths, standing in the doorway. "Am I putting you out?"

Strictly speaking he was, but the fact that he was quite dashing, in a navy-blue suit, looking like a better-groomed version of Ross Poldark, made Hailey feel that she could overlook the inconvenience.

She smiled.

"How can I help?"

He smiled back.

"I'm after a book."

"Well, you're in the right place," she replied, gesturing to the bookshelves.

He laughed and rolled his eyes.

"Maybe I should be more specific. It's my mum's birthday. I'd forgotten until about ten minutes ago, and I will not be her favourite son if I don't get her a little something."

"I understand. It's very important to remain her favourite son. What she does she like reading? Does she have any favourite authors?"

"She taught English before she retired, so she has bookshelves full of the classics," he explained. "I'm not really sure what she reads for pleasure, though. Books of the moment, I think."

He frowned, as if trying to remember something.

"She mentioned reading something by that guy who used to do 'Pointless'."

Hailey nodded.

"Right, so she probably likes mysteries. I think I might have the perfect book for her."

"Brilliant. Where is it?"

"Don't worry. I'll find it for you."

Hailey walked to the back of the shop, scanned the shelves and pulled out a hardback book.

Illustration by Shutterstock.

"I'm afraid I don't have this in paperback. Is that a problem for you?"

"No, not at all," he replied. "You've got me out of a hole."

She walked to the till.

"Is there anything else? We have cards here on the counter, , and I do offer a gift-wrapping service, too."

"Is there anything you don't do?" He raised an eyebrow and grinned at her.

Hailey could feel her cheeks growing hot under his gaze.

"If you could wrap up the book, that would be brilliant," he added. "I'll just have a quick look at the cards."

Willing herself to remain calm and professional, she pulled out a sheet of paper and set to wrapping the book up neatly.

"Would you like me to add a bow?" she asked.

"That would be lovely. And here's the card." He put it down on the counter.

"That's one of my favourites," Hailey told him, looking at it. "I love peacocks."

"So does my mum."

She stuck the bow on then put the book and card into a bag.

"I hope she likes it."

"I'm sure she will. I'll let you know," he said. "Thank you so much."

"Not at all. Any time."

He lingered a moment, looking as if he might say something else, and then turned and left.

As the doorbell tinkled behind him, Hailey exhaled, hardly aware that she had been holding her breath.

He was gorgeous, and he was the first man who had made her heart flutter since things went wrong with Pete.

But she knew nothing about him, not even his name. He could be married for all she knew.

No, it had been a lovely moment but, in all likelihood, that's how it would remain.

She would probably never see him again.

• • • •

In spite of herself, over the next week, Hailey's heart leapt every time a customer appeared.

By the time another week had gone, she was approaching a state of equilibrium, having counselled herself to be sensible and not act like a teenager in the throes of a first crush.

One lunchtime the doorbell tinkled while she was in the stock-room.

"I'll be with you in a moment!" she called.

Her assistant, Veronica, had gone on her lunch break so there was no-one on the shop floor.

She emerged and stood stock still when she saw who was standing looking at the books.

"Hello," he said, smiling tentatively.

"Hello." Her mouth was suddenly very dry. "How can I help you?"

"I've come for a book."

She smiled.

"Well, you're in the right place."

She hoped he would remember that's what she said the first time.

He laughed.

"Just like before."

Her heart leapt.

"Who's the lucky recipient this time?" Hailey asked.

She hoped he wouldn't say it was for his wife or girlfriend.

"Me." He squirmed a little under her gaze. "The thing is, I'm not really . . ."

"Much of a reader?" she supplied.

"How did you know?" His quizzical tone and wide eyes betrayed his surprise.

"I've been doing this job for a long time," Hailey admitted. "I can pretty much work out what genre people enjoy from looking at them or maybe just asking the right questions.

"I can also tell who loves reading and who doesn't." She paused. "It is quite unusual to get someone who doesn't love books buying them unless it's for someone else."

"Well," he said, looking down at his shoes and then up again, "I thought it was about time that I did something that was good for me."

"Reading does have many benefits, but there's not much point reading if you don't enjoy it," Hailey pointed out. "Did you like reading when you were younger?"

"With an English teacher mother, I always had a bedtime story and I liked those well enough. But I didn't like reading at school. We were always forced to read what the teacher chose or what the exam board thought was amazing, and it just didn't do it for me."

"So you won't be wanting fiction then."

Hailey put her head to one side.

"OK, I'm thinking a biography or an autobiography might be just the thing for you. Follow me."

She led the way to a large collection of hardback books.

"I'm thinking maybe something about your favourite music artist, or possibly a sportsperson."

"Wow! You are amazing! I love music."

She shrugged.

"I aim to please. There's loads to choose from. Just browse away."

"I will." He paused. "What's your name?"

"Hailey."

"Hailey," he repeated, and she loved the way it sounded when he spoke it. "Thank you, Hailey. I'm Matt."

He extended his hand, and she took it.

"I'm very pleased to make your acquaintance."

She was very pleased to make his acquaintance, too, but the tinkling of the doorbell brought her out of her trance, and she excused herself to go and help the new customer.

In a way, it was a relief to advise one of her regulars on which of the latest romances she would probably enjoy most.

It gave her the opportunity to compose herself and regain her equilibrium.

He was still looking at the shelves and browsing when the transaction had been completed.

"Have you decided yet?" she asked from the safety of the counter.

"Yes, I think I'll take this one on Freddie Mercury."

He wandered over and handed the book to her.

"Good choice. I love Queen. There's something magical about them, don't you think?" Hailey asked.

"Exactly." Matt nodded. "I was indoctrinated by my parents, so a lot of what they listened to I listened to, and I just grew up loving it."

"It was very similar for me."

He shuffled a little and cleared his throat.

"Hailey. Do you think you might be interested in –"

The doorbell tinkled again very loudly.

"I'm back, my lovely. It's freezing out there."

Veronica's timing couldn't have been worse.

Matt blushed, stopped what he was saying and tapped his card on the machine.

"I'll go and hang my coat up," Veronica said. "Won't be a tick."

She bustled past, nodding to Matt as she went.

"I hope you enjoy it," Hailey said as she gave him the book in a paper bag.

She was also hoping he would finish what he had been saying.

"I'm sure I will. Bye for now."

He strolled towards the door and left without a backwards glance.

"What was that, Hailey?" Veronica asked.

"I think he was going to ask me something, but you coming back threw things a bit."

"Oh, I am sorry. Was he going to ask you out, do you think?"

"I don't know for sure."

"But you wouldn't say no?" Veronica's eyes twinkled. "He's a nice-looking chap, I'll say that. If I were a few years younger –"

"You'd still be too old for him. Anyway, I saw him first."

Veronica laughed.

"Don't worry. He'll be back."

The question was when?

• • • •

The following Saturday, Hailey stood for a moment gazing out of the shop window, watching the world pass by.

There were the dedicated shoppers, clearly on a mission to get round the supermarkets as quickly as possible before heading home, while others were content to wander the streets, enjoying their weekend and pausing occasionally to look at displays.

The shop was quiet, and she really fancied a cappuccino from the café up the road.

Maybe she would buy a cookie, too. Veronica could manage the shop for 20 minutes or so.

"Fancy a coffee, Veronica? I could just nip out while it's quiet if you're happy to keep an eye on things."

"Make that a hot chocolate and you're on. There's a chill in the air. It's a good day for a brisk walk."

Hailey thought it would be rather lovely to get out and about with Matt, but there wasn't much chance of that if he didn't come back to the shop.

She couldn't find him on the basis of a first name only acquaintance and knowing he liked music.

He must work somewhere local for him to have run to the shop before closing, but there were loads of offices in the vicinity.

Anyway, she wasn't absolutely sure he was going to ask her out. He could have been about to ask her anything.

She sighed and went to get her coat and scarf.

As Hailey joined the shoppers, she shivered. Thankfully the café wasn't that far away.

She pushed open the door and joined a queue of three people.

She looked around while she was waiting.

The tables were occupied with people of varying ages enjoying a Saturday morning treat.

One little girl was pleading with her parents for something.

"Please, Daddy. Please, say we can go."

Hailey half-watched to see what the outcome would be, and as the child's father turned his head and his face became visible, she froze.

There was no mistaking who that was, even if he wasn't wearing a suit.

She looked more closely at the woman he was with.

Blonde, beautiful, stylish – everything she wasn't.

Of course, someone like Matt would have a gorgeous wife.

Her heart sank and she felt her nose prickle, which meant tears weren't that far away.

Unwilling to be recognised or cry in public, she left the queue, slipped out of the café and ran as fast as she could, trying to dodge shoppers.

When she got back to the shop, she burst through the door.

"Where's my hot chocolate, then?" Veronica asked, looking up. "Oh, my. What's happened to you?"

Veronica's sympathetic tone was enough to provoke tears and Hailey wiped them away as quickly as they fell.

"I've been stupid, that's all."

"How have you been stupid?"

"Reading too much into something. For having too active an imagination. I saw Matt in the café – with his wife and daughter, all cosied up together."

Veronica frowned.

"That doesn't seem to fit with what you told me."

"No, it doesn't, does it? Seems like I'm just attracted to the wrong people."

"Not everyone's like Pete, you know."

"That's what I was hoping." Hailey sighed. "It looks like I was mistaken. Again.

"I'm going to the stock-room. I need to be by myself for a while."

"OK. If there's anything I can do, you know where I am," Veronica told her.

Hailey smiled weakly at her.

She spent the next hour or so trying not to think about how Matt had looked at her, how he had sounded as she thought he was about to ask her out.

Was her judgement really so skewed? She tried to focus on some administrative jobs but to no avail.

Maybe it would be better to be back in the shop.

It sounded like there were several customers in based on what Veronica was saying.

She found a mirror in her handbag and had a quick look.

She was a bit pale, but there were no streaks of mascara down her cheeks or anything like that.

She applied her lip gloss and, taking a deep breath, she went back into the shop.

What she hadn't expected was to see Matt and his daughter standing near the children's picture book stand.

When he saw her, his face lit up and he smiled warmly.

She looked around for his wife, but she was nowhere to be seen.

She looked at Veronica, who shook her head and shrugged before her attention was claimed by a customer.

Hailey was tempted to bolt back into the stock-room but that wouldn't solve anything.

There was no way she was in the mood to smile back at him, but she did want to get to the bottom of things, though speaking to him with a child present was going to be tricky.

"May I help?" she asked coolly. He frowned.

"Erm, we've come for a book, haven't we, Lottie?"

"Yes." Lottie looked up and beamed.

She was the image of Matt, with the same dark, wavy hair and brown eyes.

"Well, there's plenty to choose from."

"We were wondering if you might be able to advise us, weren't we, Lottie?"

The little girl nodded vigorously and looked expectantly at Hailey.

Well, this was awkward.

"If you'd be happy to wait for my colleague, Veronica, I'm sure she'll be able to help you. She's very good when it comes to children's books."

Matt frowned and shook his head slightly.

"And you aren't?"

Her shoulders sagged and she sighed. She would be honest.

He probably wouldn't come in here again after today anyway.

"I just think it would be best. I thought you . . . but I obviously misunderstood. I saw you earlier in the café."

She looked directly at him, watching for his reaction.

Matt frowned, then he smiled.

"It wasn't me you saw. That was my twin brother, who is happily married to Lottie's mum. They are visiting this weekend."

"What?"

"Lottie. Can you tell the nice book lady who I am?"

"He's my Uncle Matt, and he looks just like Daddy," Lottie declared. "Everybody mixes them up all the time. But I don't."

She shook her head vigorously, proud that she could tell the difference.

Hailey looked from one to the other. Sometimes truth was stranger than fiction.

"Can you help me choose a book, please? Uncle Matt said he would buy me one for being a good girl while Mummy and Daddy go out."

"I'm sure I can manage that." Hailey grinned. "I'm guessing you like animals. Would I be right?"

"Yes, I love them. I really want a dog as a pet, but Mummy won't let me."

"Well, how about we find you a book with a dog in it instead?"

Lottie jumped up and down.

"Yes, please."

Hailey looked at the stand and pulled out a couple of books that she thought would suit.

She read the blurbs to Lottie, who listened very carefully.

"I can't decide, Uncle Matt.

"Could I have both? Please!"

"You have got me wrapped round your little finger, Charlotte Adams. You'll have to be extra good if I'm getting you two."

"Thank you!"

"Do you want to have a look at the bookmarks, Lottie?" Hailey asked. "Maybe I can give one of those to you as a present."

"Really? Oh, thank you."

She raced off to the counter where Veronica brought the box of bookmarks down to her level so she could choose.

"That's very kind of you," Matt murmured.

"Well, how else was I going to get a word with you on my own?" Hailey tilted her head and raised an eyebrow.

Matt ran his hand through his hair.

"So do you think you might be interested in a drink some time, or even dinner?" He cleared his throat.

Hailey grinned.

"Well, now we've cleared up the misunderstanding, I think I might be interested in both."

"How about a drink after work on Monday and we'll go from there?"

"Sounds perfect."

She wished for a moment that they were the only two people in the shop and that he would kiss her. But Monday wasn't far away.

As if reading her mind, he reached for her hand and gave it a gentle squeeze.

"Till Monday, then." ◾

WINNIE THE BEAR

DR HARRY COLEBOURN, a Canadian veterinarian, purchased a bear cub in 1914 and named her Winnie after his hometown of Winnipeg.

Winnie became a beloved mascot for the Canadian troops. She accompanied Colebourn to England, where she captured the heart of a boy: Christopher Robin Milne.

After the war, Harry donated Winnie to the London Zoo. There she became a beloved attraction, often visited by the Milne family. Christopher Robin was fond of Winnie, and his experiences with the bear inspired his father, A.A. Milne, to create the beloved character of Winnie-the-Pooh.

Winnie's legacy lives on in the work of A.A. Milne and in two statues – one in Winnipeg and one in London Zoo.

Image: Shutterstock.

At Your Service

BY CHARMAINE FLETCHER

T was dark when Lilith Fielding reached Carfax Hall. The moon, a bright pearl, hung low against the swirling sky, illuminating trees fringing the undulating landscape around the house.

Approaching the imposing stairs to the oak door, Lilith glanced up at the edifice – her home for the next few weeks – wondering what she might find inside.

"I'm most grateful to you for stepping in so quickly and helping us while Mrs Morgan, my usual housekeeper, is away," Lady Enderby said when they met the next day.

"When her sister suddenly became ill," she added, "there was nobody else. To be honest, it was rather a nuisance. Still, it can't be helped. Besides, you're here now, Mrs Fielding."

She smiled frostily, using Lilith's courtesy title.

"Thank you. I'll do everything I can." Lilith nodded graciously.

"Yes, the agency said as much. Although you're not quite what I was expecting," Lady Enderby admitted as Lilith tucked a stray curl inside her bonnet. "Now, I must get on . . ."

Their discussion evidently over, Lilith watched Lady Enderby tug a bell-pull by the fireplace.

"Snubb, our butler, will introduce you to the downstairs staff," Lady Enderby said, waving her hand dismissively as Snubb, a suave man in his forties, appeared.

Meandering through Carfax Hall's shadowy passages, Lilith observed the portraits lining the walls, faces disapproving, eyes following them.

Then Snubb asked Lilith about her previous posts.

"Well, I've been fairly itinerant actually." She smiled, with a sidelong glance. "Berwick, Bideford, Norwich, Pendle – all historic places. In fact, wherever I might be useful."

"Very commendable, I'm sure," he replied approvingly on reaching the kitchen. "Now, my office is over here and Mrs Morgan's – or rather your, sitting-room is next door.

"The kitchen's through there." He indicated. "Mrs Murdle and the others will be waiting to meet you."

"Nice, are they?" Lilith asked casually.

"That's a matter of opinion," Snubb replied. "The parlourmaid, Rosie, is a good, willing girl, but I don't mind saying certain maids

Illustration: Sailesh Thakrar.

Set in
the late
1800s

do put upon her somewhat. It's a shame because she's a diligent young thing and quite fond of Leonard, our first footman.

"Both have the makings of excellent senior servants, too."

"Indeed," Lilith replied as they entered the kitchen, surveying the staff lined up to greet her.

As they were introduced, Mrs Murdle bobbed an awkward curtsy, nudging her kitchen maid Ivy who, stifling a giggle, did likewise.

Behind stood Marcia and Bridget, the chambermaids. Both gave an impression of dignity and decorum, Lilith thought.

Yet beyond feigned deference, she saw a malicious glint or two lurking.

"Where's Rosie?" Mr Snubb asked, frowning.

"Sir, she offered to do the bedrooms this morning, the shoes as well. Marcia thinks she's coming down with something and polish brings on her bronchitis," Bridget volunteered, giving Marcia a knowing glance, Lilith noticed.

"Well, I hope she's better by the Hallowe'en dance in the village," Lilith replied smoothly. "It wouldn't do to suffer a chest complaint, especially on a foggy October night."

"I wasn't aware you knew about that," Mr Snubb said, sounding surprised.

"Oh, I saw a poster while travelling to the Hall. Apparently it's on the same Saturday when I depart and the esteemed Mrs

Morgan returns."

"The maids always go to the Hallowe'en dance – it's tradition." Marcia glared, adding a cough for good measure.

"Perhaps, but permission isn't obligatory," Lilith responded firmly, staring hard at the girl, her green eyes glittering intensely despite the dimly lit kitchen.

The two maids glanced at one another, she noticed, their mouths narrowing into mean, thin lines.

"Come on, then," Lilith said suddenly, clapping her hands, breaking the silence. "The morning is nearly over and I have work for you, Marcia. It's something perfect for an ailing chest."

Soon they found themselves in the laundry, batting their way through soapy vapour, the scent of carbolic and lavender filling the air.

"I spoke to the laundry staff, Bessie and Agnes, earlier," Lilith began. "It seems, as there were guests at the weekend, they need extra help –"

"But . . ." Marcia started to say.

Lilith raised her hand.

"I know – being a humble chambermaid, you don't feel up to their high professional standards, but pounding a nice, steamy dolly tub will benefit your lungs enormously.

"No, don't thank me," Lilith trilled breezily, turning on her heel to leave before Marcia could protest.

"There you are, Rosie," Mrs Murdle said later. "I've prepared tea, cake, crumpets and sandwiches for Mrs Fielding, though 'tis an odd sort of lunch if you ask me."

The parlourmaid collected the tray and left to deliver it.

"Ah, come in." Lilith smiled, shortly afterwards.

"Have you eaten yet, my dear?" she asked when Rosie set down her lunch.

"N-no, I haven't," she stammered, flushing. "Bridget asked me to run an errand in the village, so I didn't have time."

"Then why not join me? There's plenty for two."

Rosie glanced towards the door.

"Don't worry. I'm in charge now," Lilith said, removing the lid from a dish of warm muffins and handing Rosie a plate.

"Now, let's chat a little about your life here at Carfax Hall – especially regarding Marcia and Bridget," she added smoothly.

Before long, Rosie revealed that she was treated as a lackey by the older girls who, to Lilith's chagrin, took advantage of her willingness and good nature.

". . . and they're better paid than me." Rosie continued. "I know that's only right, them being chambermaids, but I do most of their work, too – even emptying the chamber pots!"

"I thought as much." Lilith nodded. "Tell me – do you wish to attend the Hallowe'en dance later this month?"

"Oh, yes, Mrs Fielding," Rosie replied, swallowing some éclair, "but Bridget and Marcia say I'll be needed here. I was supposed to be dancing with Master Edward, too – his lordship's heir.

"Only I was sent to turn down the beds instead. When I got back, all the fun was over," she finished mournfully.

"What happens at this Hallowe'en affair in the village – dancing, naturally, anything else?" Lileth asked.

"Yes," Rosie replied dreamily. "We have food and games, like ducking for apples, snapdragon and 'guising'.

"That's popular here, too, being so far north," she explained, her lilting accent alight with excitement. "Village children dress in costumes, singing songs or telling stories and receive a penny or toffee apple from the grown-ups.

"In between, there's dancing – my favourite part. I've been learning the steps to new dances from a book Master Edward left in the library.

"Mrs Morgan said I could – when I'm not working, of course. Then, we have what's called 'soul cake', spiced shortbread, while watching a bonfire on the village green."

"A bonfire, really, on Hallowe'en of all things," Lilith observed faintly.

"So presumably, you attended last year?" she continued.

"No, I didn't," Rosie confessed. "Marcia and Bridget said it wasn't right that three maids should go, when the beds needed doing. Being more senior, they went instead.

"I heard about it from them afterwards, mind. It sounded wonderful. I've thought of little else but going ever since – not that I shall, though, I expect," Rosie admitted sadly.

"I see." Lilith smiled sternly. "Well, perhaps this time it will be different."

She reached for her voluminous carpetbag and produced a small, leather book.

"'Practical Invocations For Everyday Success'," Rosie read, her face puzzled.

"I bought this many years ago from a rather quaint bookshop," Lilith explained. "Apparently, eastern sages call them 'mantras'.

"Trust me, they work."

"Isn't dabbling in such things dangerous?" Rosie remarked, examining it curiously.

"No. It's simply the acquisition of confidence, you know – 'mind over matter', with herbs thrown in!" Lilith laughed. "Borrow it. See what you think – but I'll need it back before I go."

• • • •

Two days later, Rosie watched Bridget being admonished by Snubb for disposing of some work papers Lord Enderby had left in his bedroom.

"It was an accident, Mr Snubb!" Bridget cried, chin jutting defiantly. "They were badly crumpled with scribbles on, so I threw them in the bin!"

"His lordship is livid, and it's all your fault, you silly girl!" Mr Snubb fumed.

"Excuse me, sir, but are these what you're looking for?" Rosie asked, handing the butler a sheaf of smoothed-out paper.

"Only I recognised the writing, seeing as I clean his lordship's study and thought they might be important," she finished, quickly glancing at Lilith who winked approvingly at her.

"Well done, Rosie!" Snubb said. "Your swift thinking has utterly saved the day! I believe Lady Enderby's maid is leaving to get married next year. In view of this, I thought Mrs Fielding might wish to suggest that she trains you as her replacement."

"A lady's maid?" Bridget protested, outraged.

"That should be me, or at least Marcia –" she began but, eyeing the paperwork pointedly, Lilith interrupted her.

"I disagree," she insisted firmly. "You're too impulsive. Besides, Marcia's skin reaction to nothing more than a little soap renders her unsuitable for looking after fine clothing.

"I'll speak to her ladyship immediately," Lilith added.

•   •   •   •

"Well?" Lilith asked as Rosie brought her coffee the next day.

"I got it." Rosie smiled. "Bridget was the obvious choice, but after that business with his lordship's papers, they needed someone industrious, reliable and with more common sense.

"Only . . . I cheated," she admitted, looking shamefaced.

"How?" Lilith asked.

"By using your special book to get a better position, but that also punished Marcia and Bridget. Marcia has a nasty rash from laundry work. Next, Bridget made a mistake and will probably stay a chambermaid forever .

"Could I really be a witch of sorts, Mrs Fielding?"

"Maybe my book did work, but sometimes we make our own magic, too," Lilith soothed.

"I don't understand." Rosie frowned.

"You simply did the appropriate thing exactly when required and Mr Snubb realised your potential.

Meanwhile, Marcia and Bridget showed themselves to be inept, lazy and arrogant. Who else would he have chosen?"

"Maybe," Rosie agreed.

Smiling, Lilith saw the girl's chin rise a notch, her confidence growing.

"Incidentally, I have tickets for the Hallowe'en dance next Saturday," Lilith told her. "It seems Marcia's unable to attend, and with Bridget in disgrace, they're both crying off.

"Why not take your chance and go? I can't promise Master Edward, but I heard Leonard, that rather personable young footman, will be there . . ." she teased.

"Something tells me you're going to be enchanted," she added mischievously.

When Lilith eventually left, Rosie saw her off at the local train station, before going to the Hallowe'en dance afterwards.

Having returned the housekeeper's book earlier, they bid each other a fond goodbye.

"I'll never forget you, Mrs Fielding," Rosie said tearfully.

"Nor I you." Lilith smiled. "Now remember: pare that apple at midnight and throw the peel over your shoulder to reveal your true love's initial.

"I sense the letter 'L' might just appear," she finished as, reluctantly waving farewell, Rosie walked with a new lightness of step towards the exit, where Leonard waited.

Disappearing down the misty platform, silhouetted against the fading, fiery embers of the October sunset, Lilith's eyes twinkled – a job well done. ▪

National Short Person Day

In my stocking soles I'm not quite five feet,
Trying to reach top shelves leaves me downbeat!
My shoe size is merely a tiny size two,
Limiting my choices to very few!
Finding trousers to fit is an impossible quest;
They're always too long and I get very stressed.
I try wearing heels to make me look tall,
But folks still say, "Oh, you're very small".
At the shows and concerts I go to see
The tallest person always sits in front of me!
But it isn't always doom and gloom:
I don't have to worry about extra leg room.
The best things come in small packages, they say, so
Let's celebrate National Short Person Day!

By Sharon Haston

Illustration: Shutterstock.

Today's Battles

BY TESS NILAND KIMBER

JILLY wondered how Mrs Chester did this every year. She was shivering in the November chill, despite her padded jacket, scarf and gloves.

At least standing in the local supermarket's porch was a good pitch.

A little girl slipped money into Jilly's collecting tin.

"Thank you. What would you like? A paper poppy to pin on your coat or a wristband?" Jilly asked the little girl, who was standing with a tall, dark-haired man.

"A paper one, please. Can I choose, Daddy?" she asked, pointing to the box of identical red poppies.

"Of course," her dad replied.

"Are they recyclable?" he then asked Jilly.

She nodded.

"Oh, yes. Obviously, the poppy and leaf are paper, but the stem and centre are made from fully biodegradable plastic."

"I hope you didn't mind me asking." He smiled, his warm brown eyes holding hers.

"Not at all." She smiled back.

She had loved meeting so many friendly people on her first stint as a poppy collector, and this man was no exception.

"Actually, I have been asked the same question several times," she told him.

"Daddy, please can you pin the poppy on my coat?" his daughter asked politely.

As he stooped to do so, there was a sudden yell.

"Stop that woman!"

Jilly looked up as a teenage girl with blue hair dashed by, carrying tins and a loaf of bread squashed in her arms.

She wondered why her shopping wasn't in a bag, then understood – she was shoplifting!

Quickly, Jilly passed her collecting tin to the dad and chased after the girl.

"Stop!" she called.

Jilly loved running. Every Saturday she attended the local parkrun, and since splitting from David she'd joined the Tuesday Nighters, a local running group who met for fun runs around the town.

Getting into her stride, Jilly gained on the girl.

Illustration: Shutterstock.

They weaved through the car park, and when they reached the traffic lights, Jilly suddenly feared that the girl might take her chances and dart across the busy road.

Lunging forward, Jilly reached out and caught hold of the girl's arm.

"Hey! Get off!" the girl shouted, glaring as she dropped the items she was carrying.

But Jilly held on and the girl soon stopped struggling.

"What are you doing?" Jilly demanded.

She expected the girl to swear, or maybe even try to fight her off, but instead she burst into tears.

"I'm so hungry!" she cried, tears streaming down her dirty face. "I haven't done anything like this before."

A security guard gasped behind them, beads of sweat decorating his forehead.

"Right! You had better come

> with me."

Jilly was still clasping the girl's thin wrist.

"Go easy on her. There might be more to this."

The security guard raised his eyebrows before taking hold of the girl.

"Maybe," he conceded, "although you would be surprised how many sob stories we hear."

Jilly nodded as she picked up the discarded items from the pavement before following the security guard and the girl back to the supermarket.

She only hoped Daisy's dad hadn't minded watching her collection tin and box of poppy merchandise while she'd helped apprehend the girl.

As they walked, she heard snippets of the girl's conversation with the security guard.

"Hungry . . . no money – Universal Credit late. Didn't mean to."

Her heart ached for the teenager.

Jilly knew only too well that not everyone was lucky enough to have a warm, happy home.

Of course, stealing was wrong, but she hoped the supermarket manager would at least listen to the girl's story.

Once back at the supermarket, Jilly watched the security guard and the girl, who was now walking calmly beside him, enter the store.

"Wow! You ran like the wind," Daisy's dad said to Jilly when she returned to her spot in the supermarket's porch.

"Luckily I'm wearing my running shoes." She grinned.

"Mrs Chester – the neighbour I'm standing in for – said poppy collecting is hard on the feet. But I do feel sorry for that young girl."

The man sighed.

"We have an awful lot of shoplifters here," he told her sadly.

"Oh, do you work here?" she asked, thanking him as she took back the box and collecting tin.

"Yes, I'm the manager of the supermarket, although it's my weekend off," he explained. "I only see Daisy every other week, so I make sure I book the time off."

"Oh, right." Jilly smiled. "Well, I hope whoever's standing in for you today will give the girl the benefit of the doubt. Life's hard for people right now."

A smart gentleman and his wife put some change in her collecting tin as they passed by.

Distracted, she concentrated on handing them their poppies.

When she looked up, Daisy and her dad had disappeared.

It was a shame; she'd enjoyed talking to them.

Thinking of the girl with the blue hair again, she sighed, hoping she wouldn't see the police arrive any time soon.

She wondered if she'd ever find out if the store had treated her leniently.

She wasn't being nosy; she just cared. It was her job, she supposed.

For the last five years Jilly had been working as a social worker.

"There you are," she said to the couple, handing them pins to attach their poppies to their coats.

"Thank you," the man replied. "I always think of my comrades at this time of year. I fought in the Falklands war. I'll never forget it."

Jilly nodded and smiled.

After they'd gone, she studied the noticeboards around her collecting table.

There were some large black and white photographs of young men who'd fought in both World Wars I, with other full-colour shots of soldiers who'd been in more recent conflicts like the man she'd just met.

Some servicemen had less obvious injuries, while others were seated in wheelchairs.

Her heart went out to them and she hoped this year they would collect record levels of funds.

But as she gazed at the posters, she realised that although today's youngsters thankfully didn't have a war to fight, they faced other battles.

Like the mum she had helped last week who'd been left by her partner to care for five children, or the lady with early onset Parkinson's who was determined to stay in her home for as long as possible but who only had one family member living at the other end of the country.

And, of course, the teenage girl with the blue hair who she'd chased this morning.

What hardships was she battling?

Her thoughts were broken when she heard a voice beside her.

"That's all sorted."

Jilly turned. It was Daisy's dad.

"Sorted?" She frowned.

"The girl who ran off with the shopping," he explained. "She agreed to return the goods and we've given her information on how to access the local food bank."

Jilly smiled.

"That's so kind. Thank you."

● ● ● ● ●

Over the next few days, Jilly grew to know Sion – Daisy's dad.

Sometimes he'd pop out with a hot chocolate for her; other days he'd spend his break chatting to her, and once he'd even offered her a lift home.

"Is that guy your boyfriend?" a voice asked one day as Sion disappeared inside the store to start work again.

Jilly looked up to find the girl with the blue hair staring at her.

"Oh, no," she replied. "I only know him through collecting here for the Poppy Appeal over the last few days."

"Right," the girl said with a steady gaze.

Jilly wasn't sure what she wanted.

"Look," she began, "about the other day . . ."

"Yeah." The girl sniffed. "That's what I'm here about. I wanted to say cheers and all that. For helping. I thought I'd be in a lot of trouble, but what you said must've helped, so thanks."

Jilly smiled.

"Well, thank you for taking the trouble to come back and say that. I appreciate it. I hope you're getting help now."

"Yeah, a bit." The girl turned to leave but Jilly called her back.

"Here – take this," she said,

handing her a poppy wristband.

"But I . . ."

Jilly put up her hand.

"No, I want you to have it."

The girl nodded.

"Oh, please thank your boyfriend, too. He put in a good word for me."

"He's not my boyfriend," Jilly repeated.

"No? Well, he will be soon. I can tell." The girl grinned.

As she watched the young girl slip on the wristband, Jilly put some money in the tin for her and wondered if she was right.

Well, if she was, she wouldn't mind that at all . . .

• • • •

"If you're a social worker, how come you have time to collect for the Poppy Appeal?" Sion asked Jilly one day.

His brown eyes held hers as he handed her a welcome hot chocolate.

"I'm on annual leave. I was going to North Macedonia with my boyfriend – or rather ex – but we split a couple of months ago," Jilly explained. "By the time I was refunded, I didn't fancy the remaining holidays.

"When my neighbour hurt her leg, she was so worried about letting down the Legion that I suggested I use some of my days off to collect."

"That's kind. I've not met many young collectors." Sion smiled. "Don't you feel like you've missed out on a break, though?"

No, Jilly wanted to say, because I've met you.

For a second, the girl with the blue hair's words came back to her and she blushed.

Sion was everything she liked – tall with warm brown eyes and, most importantly, he cared.

But she didn't say this.

"Well, I've had some great days out when I've not been collecting," she said instead. "I've visited two theme parks – I love rollercoasters."

"Really?" Sion replied. "So do I! The scarier the better."

"My ex hated rides, so it's good to do something I enjoy for a change."

"I wish I'd known you were going. I love all that stuff, but it's more fun with someone."

"Well, I'm off to Alton Towers later this week," Jilly told him, surprising herself. "You're welcome to join me. If you want to, that is."

A young woman with a toddler in a pushchair put money in her tin then.

As she helped the lady, her cheeks burned.

Had she really just suggested to Sion they go out?

By the time she turned back to Sion, she felt completely embarrassed.

"Sorry, I shouldn't have –"

"I'd love to! When are you going?" he asked.

Jilly sighed with relief as they arranged to meet on Thursday.

"Well, I'd better do some work, or I'll have to sack myself." He grinned. "I'm really looking forward to Thursday."

"Me, too," Jilly replied.

And as she watched him walk back into the supermarket, she thought that even though North Macedonia had sounded fantastic, this holiday was turning into her best one yet!

TOMBILI THE CAT

TURKEY'S cities are renowned for free-roaming feline residents. For centuries, they've co-existed with humans, becoming an integral part of Turkish urban culture. Individuals and local authorities alike contribute to the wellbeing of these beloved companions.

One such feline celebrity was Tombili. Her iconic pose, captured and shared online, turned her into a sensation. Nicknamed Tombili (meaning "chubby" in Turkish), she became a symbol of the street's relaxed lifestyle.

Following her passing, a heartfelt public campaign led to the erection of a statue in her memory. Unfortunately the statue was stolen a month later, but at the end the thieves relented, returning it to its rightful place.

Image: Johannes Nickel/Wikimedia Commons

Where It All Began

BY LYNDA FRANKLIN

THERE is something about Christmas that takes our minds back to Christmases gone by. Maybe it's because the past is safe.

We can choose to remember the good things – the things that made us happy.

Yet sometimes the past is elusive. Sometimes it's hard or even impossible to connect with the past.

That's the reason I've travelled to York. I'm here to recapture a part of my life I know little about.

It was a week before Christmas on the day I went.

The Christmas market was in full flow and the streets were packed to bursting.

It was almost impossible to move either forwards or backwards as crowds of people descended on this lovely city.

The pavements were alive with music and noise, and pungent smells of cooking wafted in the air from a multitude of stalls.

The weather forecast hadn't been too bad. It was bitterly cold, of course, but Yorkshire always is.

No snow was forecast.

I could have driven, perhaps, but it was a long way.

In the end I booked a seat on the train – two seats actually, because Darren insisted on coming with me.

I had decided to come alone, but he's been so good over the years, so understanding of the way I feel, that I didn't have the heart to tell him.

So we booked a room at a B&B in the heart of York and came together.

The B&B was warm, welcoming and decked in decorations.

A huge tree stood in the foyer with fake presents underneath.

There were raffle tickets to buy for charity on the desk, together with a big, opened tin of chocolates for anyone to help themselves.

There was tinsel, lights, garlands – all designed to make the guests feel happy and full of Christmas spirit.

I wouldn't allow myself to relax yet. There was something I had to do first.

We booked in and made our way to our room on the second floor.

"Nice." Darren said.

He never wasted words, which was probably why we got on so well.

I watched him lie back on the

Illustration: Mandy Dixon.

bed with a contented groan.

"Cup of tea?" I picked up the kettle from the tea tray. "It looks like we've got biscuits, too."

"Yeah, I'm dying for a cuppa. I'm frozen stiff."

"I know. It's bitter out there."

We could have taken a taxi from the station, but we decided to walk.

It had taken three long hours on the train, and I told Darren I was desperate to stretch my legs and feel fresh air on my face.

Neither of us had bargained on it being so sharply cold.

"Kettle's boiling," I said automatically.

We drank tea and ate most of the biscuits, gradually warming up and feeling sleepy after our long journey.

But I didn't want to rest. I couldn't rest.

I'd promised myself this visit and now I wanted to experience and soak in every detail.

"I've got a message from Ann," I said, looking at my phone.

"What does she say?"

"She suggests eleven a.m. tomorrow."

"Good not too early."

"We can have a leisurely breakfast and then walk there. It should only take fifteen minutes or so."

"OK, tell her we'll be there."

I sent off a quick text and my stomach started to churn.

The next morning was just as cold, but bright with winter sun.

It streamed through the windows as we ate our breakfast, and we basked in the unnatural warmth.

"We mustn't be late," I said, pushing bacon around my plate.

"We won't be." Darren was calm and in control, and I was suddenly glad he'd come with me.

I don't know what made me think I could do this without him.

We went back to our room and pulled on coats and boots.

I wound my bright red scarf around my neck and plonked a red bobble hat on my head.

"Let's go," Darren said with a small smile.

I took a deep breath.

"Yeah, let's go."

York was pretty empty at that hour. It was hard to imagine how crowded and busy it had been the night before.

We walked briskly to keep warm, and also to make sure we arrived in time.

Ann would be wearing a green scarf and hat. She would hopefully be easy to see.

We reached the cathedral with five minutes to spare.

It looked magnificent, a beacon of beauty in the centre of a beautiful city.

The surrounding trees were hung with lights, and an impressive Christmas tree stood close by.

Darkness had previously transformed it all into glittering splendour, but by day it was simply a place that made me want to just stand and stare.

Perhaps I should consider myself fortunate to have been born in such a city.

"Alison?"

I smiled uncertainly at the older woman walking towards me.

"Yes, I'm Alison. You must be Ann."

She laughed, a warm deep laugh.

"Oh, my goodness, I can't believe it's you."

Ann was probably in her sixties, wrapped up in a brown coat with the agreed green hat on her head.

The agreed green scarf was swinging freely around her neck.

"You've changed quite a bit since I last saw you," she added in a softer voice. "Can I give you a hug?"

I stepped forward first.

"I expect I have," I said quietly.

Ann pulled away but didn't let go of my hands. "

"I've often thought about you, you know, wondered what happened to you."

"Thank you." I didn't know what else to say.

"I hope you've been happy." She looked embarrassed then, as if unsure what to say.

I nodded.

"Yes, I have. Oh – this is Darren by the way."

Darren inclined his head slightly and smiled.

"I'm so glad," she said.

"Will you show me – can you remember?" I asked her, hardly daring to say the words.

"Of course I'll show you. Do I remember? Oh, Alison, of course I remember! Follow me."

We walked into the cathedral grounds and towards the

cathedral itself.

Again I was struck by the size and grandeur of this ancient building that had watched over the city of York for centuries.

We paused outside for a mere second, before Ann led me to a sheltered corner at the back of the porch.

"Just there, Alison," she said simply.

"There?" I repeated softly, staring at the empty space.

Ann walked over and stood beside a section of wall.

"You were lying here in a cardboard box, wrapped up in a white blanket," she told me. "You were warm, but must have been hungry because you were crying. That's the only reason I noticed you.

"I picked you up." She shrugged. "I wasn't sure what to do at first."

"So you took me to the hospital?"

"I flagged down a taxi and took you straight there." Ann nodded.

"Maybe I should have called the police, but I just wanted to get you somewhere safe." She sighed softly at the memory. "The hospital called the police."

There was silence then, both of us thinking about that night 32 years ago.

Ann was first to speak.

"The nurses called you Angel because it was so near Christmas."

"I don't think I could have lived up to that name," I said wryly.

Ann chuckled.

"It might have been hard. Anyway, you already had a name. It was written on a piece of paper with your date of birth, pushed into the box with you.

"Alison Louise."

There was a slight flurry of snow in the air now after all.

Not enough to settle, but enough to make the cathedral look even more magical.

I'd been left in a place where God would watch over me until I was found.

That's what Nurse Browne told me when I managed to trace her.

She couldn't remember who had brought me to the hospital, but Ann's name was in the police records.

It was surprisingly easy to trace her.

Making the decision to come here and actually meet her had taken a while. But now was the right time.

We walked to a nearby café and sat in the welcoming warmth drinking hot chocolate.

"Has it helped coming today?" Ann asked.

I stirred my drink thoughtfully, before nodding.

"Definitely. There was always a piece of jigsaw missing before."

Ann smiled and took a sip of chocolate.

I was almost ten when my mother patted the sofa and asked me to sit down.

The fire was roaring and we'd just finished our tea.

"I've got a special story to tell you," she said.

She wove it into a beautiful tale of love and hope, explaining how the lady loved me very much, but was young and frightened and unsure how she would care for me.

"She cried as she walked away," she said. "She waited around the corner until she knew you had

165

been found."

I remember the story feeling romantic and a little exciting. The full implications of it all didn't register at all.

And then, as I got older, I began to wonder about the person who had found me.

My mother couldn't tell me anything at all, but she helped when I decided to try and trace her – because suddenly I knew I needed to meet this person.

"When is your baby due?"

"What?" I looked at Ann in surprise.

"You are pregnant, aren't you? I know the glow of a mum to be when I see one." She covered my hand with hers. "I guess that's why you needed to come today."

I nodded.

"That's exactly why."

Ann sat back and smiled.

"You'll be a great mum."

"I hope so." I passed her our little scan picture. "It's a girl."

"Oh, that's lovely." Ann stared at the picture. "You could never find out in my day, of course."

"We'd like to use your name as her middle name, if that's OK."

Ann looked surprised.

"Really? Well – I'm very honoured."

I smiled at her.

"Well – I'm very grateful."

We finished our drinks and said our goodbyes outside the café.

Ann asked me to keep in touch, and I promised I would.

Walking back to the B&B, I found myself thinking about my mother's words all those years ago.

"She cried as she walked away". That's what she'd told me.

I remember how confused I'd felt.

"How do you know?" I asked her. "How do you know she cried? You weren't even there."

Then I saw the tears in my mother's eyes and realised she was that lady.

It had been my own mother who had cried and waited round the corner to make sure I was found.

"The two days I spent without you were the longest and hardest of my entire life," she admitted. "I should have known your dad would stand by me.

"We went to the hospital together to bring you home." She pulled me towards her and held me tight. "I love you, Alison."

● ● ● ●

The B&B seemed even more warm and welcoming on our return.

"I must phone Mum and tell her how it went today," I told Darren. "She'll want to meet Ann, I know."

"We'll come back in the summer with your mum and dad," Darren said. "And Maisie Ann, of course!"

I smiled at the thought of bringing our baby daughter to York and showing her the place where I was born.

No-one can change the past. It happened.

Yet I have felt loved all my life, and Darren and I have so much more to look forward to.

I reached for his hand, placing it on my stomach.

"I felt something – a flutter."

We stood in the half light, connected to our daughter, and a sense of peace drifted over me.

Everything was finally where it was meant to be. ▣

BRACKLINN FALLS, CALLANDER.

THE Callander Crags offer a challenging yet rewarding hike, with stunning views of Loch Venachar and the surrounding countryside. The route takes you through ancient woodlands, past historic landmarks and along the dramatic Keltie Water.

The highlight of the walk is undoubtedly Bracklinn Falls, where the river cascades over a series of dramatic drops.

The power and beauty of the falls are truly awe-inspiring and can be taken in from the new bridge, opened in 2023.

The walk can be combined with a visit to the historic town of Callander, which offers a range of shops, cafés and attractions.

Those looking for a longer excursion can continue on the road into lonely and beautiful Glen Artney, away to the east of Callander and the Falls.

Change Has Come

BY TERESA ASHBY

BENNY watched as Marcie put the finishing touches to the tree in the corner of the shop window. For the first time since he was a small boy, he truly felt the wonder of Christmas.

She'd set up a model train that trundled round a snowy landscape. There was also a group of houses with lights shining from the windows.

It all looked incredibly Christmassy and welcoming.

In fact, he wouldn't mind living in that village. It had a peaceful and friendly ambience, as if you could step out of your front door and find a friendly face.

"It's a work of art, Marcie," he said, and she gave a start.

"You think it looks OK?"

"It looks brilliant," he told her.

Benny used to run the shop with his ex Stella, but after she left things had gone downhill.

He'd struggled along on his own for a couple of years, but the shop had ended up looking as tired and forlorn as he felt.

He'd decided to sell up, and filled the window with neon coloured signs saying, *Closing Down Sale! Everything Must Go!*

That was when Marcie had walked in, looking furious.

"Is this true?" she'd demanded. "Are you really closing down?"

"Yes," he replied.

"But why?" she cried. "This is the only place for miles I can buy the paints my son needs."

"It's getting too much for me," he admitted.

"I remember your wife used to work here with you," Marcie went on. "Is it true she left you?"

He was taken aback by her question.

"I'll take that as a yes," she said when he didn't reply.

He remembered her coming in regularly for paints and sometimes she'd ask him to order in a model kit for her son.

They were good customers.

Occasionally she brought the boy in with her to choose his paints or a new model.

He was a nice lad, always nicely turned out and very polite.

He'd muttered something about it being difficult to find staff and she'd scoffed.

"Difficult to find the right staff maybe," she said. "You've had a couple that weren't suited."

She wasn't wrong.

He'd tried to employ someone, but the first person didn't like

168

Illustration: Pat Gregory.

children and made no secret of the fact, which was no good when you worked in a toy shop.

The second one used to bring her children to work and let them loose on the toys. Packets were torn open, things got broken.

He felt mean asking her to leave after he tripped over a roller skate left on the floor, but she was relieved as she'd found that working in a shop wasn't for her.

"It is what it is," he'd replied to Marcie that day.

"What if I work for you?" she replied. "I can come in as soon as I've taken Zach to school and pick him up in the afternoon. He could sit do his homework or work on a model until it's time to close."

"I don't . . . I mean . . ."

"I've experience and I'm good with customers," she continued. "Zach will behave himself. I won't let you down, Mr Hope."

"Benny," he said and held out his hand. "If we're going to be working together, it ought to be on first name terms."

Marcie had smiled, ignored his hand and hugged him.

"Thank you, Benny," she said. "You're a lifesaver. I thought I'd never get another job after Bobbin's closed down. Shall I take those signs down for you?"

And that was it. He hadn't looked back.

It sounded corny, but Marcie brought a breath of fresh air to ➤

the shop, and when Zach was there he was never any trouble.

Sometimes Benny found himself helping out with model building or even the maths homework.

The shop was transformed.

Customers that had been lost began to come back and the place felt lighter, as if the light fittings had been replaced with brighter bulbs.

It was all down to Marcie.

She'd started working for him last Easter and she'd changed his life. If he'd closed the shop, he dreaded to think what he'd be doing now.

He would have had to sell his flat because finding a job wouldn't have been easy – not that it would be a bad thing.

The flat had been Stella's choice.

He'd thought they were content in their three-bedroom semi in a cosy close, but once those riverside apartments went up, she began to hanker after one.

She'd closed the shop one rainy afternoon and dragged him round to look at the show flat.

"Look at these units, Benny!"

Drawers had been pulled out and allowed to slide back in.

Doors were opened to reveal all manner of storage solutions within, and she'd stepped right inside the walk-in wardrobes.

She'd hung over the sink, marvelling at the waste disposal system, and she'd practically danced round the en suite, which seemed to have jets everywhere.

They'd stood out on the balcony looking out over the windswept river. That was when Benny began to mourn his garden.

It had been his escape, his little patch of peace and quiet.

The flats had a gym and a swimming pool for the residents, but it wasn't the same.

But he loved Stella and so he pretended to like the flat, too.

He knew she'd been restless of late, bored with the shop, bored perhaps with him. He thought the new living arrangements would make her happy, but thay hadn't.

If anything, she'd seemed even more restless after their move.

Then, one day she left work early and, when he got home, she'd gone. She had cleared out everything of hers.

In the note she left she'd said it wasn't working and she felt he probably knew that, too.

Benny had struggled to pay Stella her half of the value of the flat. He'd had to borrow money to buy her out of the shop even though he'd inherited it.

It had been in the Hope family for three generations.

He'd felt lost, hurt, abandoned.

But underneath all that there was a strong undercurrent of relief, and that made him feel guilty on top of everything else.

"Have you sorted out your Santa costume, Benny?" Marcie asked, and he realised he'd been staring at the model village, lost in his thoughts.

"Yes," he replied. "I ordered it from one of our suppliers."

"Excellent," she said. "I'll make signs for the windows and then we'll start wrapping gifts."

"I don't want to charge too much," Benny admitted. "It would be nice to think that everyone could afford to come."

He looked thoughtful.

"In fact," he added. "I don't want to charge at all."

"You can't do that," Marcie said. "You've a business to run."

"I'll sell my apartment."

"Are you mad?"

The look on her face made him laugh.

He'd done so little of that since Stella left and so much since Marcie came.

"I'd like a little place with a garden," he said. "It will be my Christmas present to me. What would you like for Christmas?"

"Me?" She laughed. "I have everything I could possibly want."

"I'll get on to the estate agent's now," Benny said resolutely, his mind made up. "I could be in my dream house by Christmas."

"Don't get your hopes up. It's only six weeks away."

But Benny's hopes were up.

They were up very high, especially when the estate agent said she had several people on her books who wanted to buy a riverside apartment.

The agent arranged an open event that weekend and Benny looked at houses while prospective buyers looked over his flat.

Two weeks later he'd agreed to buy a little terraced house with a garden at the back.

● ● ● ●

The grotto, which was little more than a curtained-off area at the back of the shop, was a great success.

A lot of people who brought their children to see Santa spent money in the shop and some said they'd had no idea t how big the selection of toys was.

Sales had been up since Marcie had come to work for him. She was so friendly and welcoming,

was it any wonder that business was booming?

During a lull, Benny nipped out to the back for a cup of tea.

He sat down at the table with Zach and watched as he worked on an intricate model.

Zach looked at him and laughed.

"I can't believe I'm making models with Santa," he said.

Benny winked at him.

"Not a word," he said, pressing his finger to his lips. "The little ones think I'm the real deal."

"Well, you are, sort of," Zach said, and his cheeks flushed.

"How do you mean?"

"You're kind," Zach explained. "And you gave Mum a chance. She loves working here."

"Really?" Benny was so pleased to hear that. He was very fond of Marcie and his feelings for her had grown recently.

But he would never ask her out for fear of frightening her away. He couldn't imagine his life without her and Zach in it, so it was best to remain friends.

Ten days before Christmas, Benny got the keys to his house.

"I can't believe this happened so quickly," Marcie said.

"Neither can I!"

Benny knew he'd been lucky.

It had been very busy time, getting rid of furniture, packing up to move and wrapping gifts for the grotto.

A year ago all that activity would have drained him, but now he felt energised.

He felt at home, even though most of his stuff was still in boxes.

The house was cosy and he felt more comfortable than he ever had in the flat.

"You seem so much happier,

Benny," Marcie observed a few days later as he stocked the shelves while singing carols. "I've never heard you sing before."

"That's because I'm so happy, Marcie," he said. "Happier than I've been in a very long time."

And then everything changed.

He'd tempted fate by saying he was happy, and fate had obligingly stepped in to put the kibosh on his new contentment.

The shop door opened then, and in walked Stella.

"I'm looking for Mr Hope," she told Marcie.

"He's there," Marcie replied.

Stella looked at Benny and guffawed with laughter.

"Why are you wearing that? You look ridiculous."

He'd forgotten he was in his Santa suit.

Benny glanced at Marcie and felt his confidence ebb away.

"I'm Father Christmas," he said, trying to sound defiant.

"I've come back just in time," Stella said. "What's happened to our flat? I found it full of young people!"

"It's not our flat, Stella," he mumbled. "It ceased to be ours when I bought your share."

"Oh, Benny, you must have known I'd come back one day," she wheedled.

Benny felt himself sinking deeper into the despair that had engulfed him.

Marcie came out from behind the counter and linked her arm through Benny's.

"Sorry, who are you?" she said.

"I'm Mrs Hope."

"Not any more," Marcie replied.

Stella laughed.

"What? Don't tell me you . . . ?

How ridiculous! Benny, she's half your age!"

"I'm nine years younger," Marcie retorted. "What of it?"

What had he become that he had to be rescued by a young woman, Benny wondered. Why couldn't he speak up for himself?

But there was nothing stopping him. He'd been in Stella's thrall when they were married, but those days were gone.

"You're not welcome here, Stella," he said firmly. "I'd like you to leave."

"You can't make me leave!"

All pretence at being sweetness and light had gone now.

"My grandparents started this shop," he said. "I bought you out."

"Don't take that tone with me!" Stella snapped.

Zach came out from the back of the shop with the model he'd just finished.

He looked bewildered.

"Who's this?" Stella said menacingly.

"I'm Zach," he said defiantly. "Why are you shouting at Mum and Benny?"

She looked from Marcie to Benny and then to Zach.

"It won't last," she said nastily. "It's not you, Benny. You weren't cut out to be a family man."

"I always wanted a family, Stella," he replied. "You were the one that didn't. Please leave. I don't want you in here when the children come in to see Santa."

Stella stormed out, and when she'd gone Benny's knees almost gave way.

"Thank you," he said.

"I never liked her," Marcie said. "If I saw her here, I used to walk past. I hope you didn't mind me insinuating we were a couple."

"Not at all." He smiled.

It had been nice to pretend that they were a couplee.

"You OK, Zach?" Benny asked.

"I am now," he said and smiled, all the uncertainty gone from his face.

And then it was back, Benny's happy feeling. Maybe he had tempted fate and fate had shown him how lucky he was.

He hurried to the grotto and got ready for the children.

He'd always loved children. His grandparents had, too.

They'd had seven, and Benny's dad was the only one interested in the shop.

Benny was an only child and he used to vow that, when he had children, there would definitely be more than one.

His parents had waited years for him to arrive and had doted on him. He knew how lucky he was to have them.

But Stella didn't like children.

She was snappy with them in the shop and Benny thought it wouldn't be fair to push for a family.

It wasn't long before he was laughing and joking with the children and giving them presents.

For some it might be the only present they got, but it was an experience to be remembered and hopefully treasured.

"What are you doing for Christmas?" Marcie asked a couple of days before the big day.

"It'll just be me."

"You can't spend Christmas alone," Marcie protested. "No-one should spend Christmas alone. It strikes me that you're the sort of man who would love a family Christmas with lots of good food and fun and games."

"It's a long time since I had one of those," he said with a chuckle.

He thought briefly of Christmas with Stella, always spent at a hotel where she'd sparkle and shine in front of the other guests like the lights on the trees and he'd sit quietly and dream of something different.

"You can spend it with me and Zach," Marcie demanded.

"What about . . . ?" he began.

"I mean, who else will be there?"

Marcie had never mentioned a significant other.

"My mother will be there," she said. "And my grandparents. I know they'd love to meet you."

"Me?"

"They call you the man that put the smile back on my face," she said in her forthright way. "Will you come?

"There'll be good food, crackers, corny jokes and board games, followed by more food."

Benny didn't know what to say.

He felt Zach tugging at his sleeve.

"Please come," he said. "I'll show you all the models I've made."

"Of course if you'd rather be on your own . . ." Marcie began.

"Yes!" he said. "Yes, I'll come! Thank you!"

She hugged him and this time he hugged her back and Zach joined in.

"I think we have something rather special, Benny," she whispered, and his arms tightened around her.

"Me too," he said.

Change had come, he thought happily, and it was good. ◼

CHATSWORTH, DERBYSHIRE

THE 12th Duke of Devonshire transforms Chatsworth House into a magical winter wonderland each year. Visitors can explore the grandeur of the Painted Hall or immerse themselves in the festive spirit of the Ante Library.

Beyond the house, the estate offers a charming Christmas market in the village of Pilsley, where visitors can find unique gifts and local delicacies. The nearby village of Baslow provides cosy accommodation and picturesque walks.

Chatsworth House is a living landmark celebrating the Devonshire family's rich history. It survives so beautifully thanks to their commitment to preservation.

Seventeen generations of the Devonshires have lived here over five centuries. In that time, they've also amassed one of Europe's finest private collections of artwork.

First published in Great Britain in 2025 by DC Thomson & Co., Ltd. Registered Office: DC Thomson & Co., Ltd., Courier Buildings, 2 Albert Square, Dundee, Scotland, DD1 9QJ; www.dcthomson. co.uk. This book is an original creation by DC Thomson.© DC Thomson & Co., Ltd. 2025. All rights reserved. EU Responsible Person for product compliance: DC Thomson & Co., Ltd., c/o Findmypast Ireland Ltd, RBK House, Irishtown, Athlone, Co. Westmeath, N37 XP52, Republic of Ireland. For product safety inquiries, contact: annuals@dcthomson.co.uk tel. +44 1382 223131.

FSC
www.fsc.org
MIX
Paper | Supporting
responsible forestry
FSC® C015559